JUMPING THE QUEUE

Mary Wesley was born as Mary Farmar in 1912 to an upper-class family and grew up a rebel who believed that she was her mother's least favourite child. Like many girls of her background, she married for escape and her first marriage, to Lord Swinfen, was brief. In 1944, she met Eric Siepmann, an unsuccessful writer whom she adored. Their relationship, which was mercurial and bohemian, lasted until his death. Having taken the pen name Wesley from the family name of Wellesley she published her first novel when she was seventy years old and went on to write a subsequent nine dazzling bestsellers, including *The Camomile Lawn*. She was awarded the CBE in the 1995 New Years honours list and died in 2002.

MARY WESLEY

Jumping the Queue

VINTAGE BOOKS
London

Published by Vintage 2006

2 4 6 8 10 9 7 5 3 1

First published in Great Britain in 1983 by
Macmillan

Vintage
Random House, 20 Vauxhall Bridge Road,
London SW1V 2SA

Random House Australia (Pty) Limited
20 Alfred Street, Milsons Point, Sydney,
New South Wales 2061, Australia

Random House New Zealand Limited
18 Poland Road, Glenfield, Auckland 10, New Zealand

Random House (Pty) Limited
Isle of Houghton, Corner of Boundary Road & Carse O'Gowrie,
Houghton, 2198, South Africa

The Random House Group Limited Reg. No. 954009
www.randomhouse.co.uk/vintage

A CIP catalogue record for this book
is available from the British Library

ISBN 9780099499152 (from Jan 2007)
ISBN 0099499150

Papers used by Random House are natural,
recyclable products made from wood grown in
sustainable forests. The manufacturing processes
conform to the environmental regulations of the
country of origin

Printed and bound in Great Britain by
Cox & Wyman Limited, Reading, Berkshire

1

All week Gus had been fussed by Matilda's unusual activity. He stomped round the house peering in through the French windows, craning his neck through open doors, eyes bright, head to one side, listening. She could hear his feet slapping on the brick path as he moved from the kitchen door to the window. Soon he would leap onto the garden table, look in, try to catch her eyes. He did this inelegant jump flapping his wings, hitting them against a chair as he strained for the table. His blue eyes met hers.

'Gus, I have to make this list, it's important.'

The gander throttled gentle anxious noises in his throat, flapped his wings, raised his head, honked.

'Shut up.' She tried to ignore him, concentrating on the list: *any trouble with the pump Peake's garage they know its vagaries. For ordinary electric work Emersons in the High Street, telephone in book in kitchen table drawer.*

Gus honked louder, slapping his feet on the wooden table.

'Shut up!' Matilda shouted without looking up. Butcher, baker, post office, garage, doctor, dentist. They won't want those. Vet – they won't need him, solicitor, bank, police. They would perhaps only need these. She checked the telephone numbers, put down her pen and went to the window.

'Oh Gus.'

He nibbled her ear, making crooning noises as she stroked his cool neck sliding her hand from his head to

5

his breast, feeling the depth of his feathers, their beauty and strength, parting them with her fingers until they touched the warm breastbone. Affected by her touch Gus excreted onto the table.

'What a way to show love.' Matilda moved away to the kitchen. Guessing which way she was going the bird jumped off the table and half ran, half walked to the kitchen door where he stood peering in, knowing he was not allowed inside the house.

Matilda ran water into a bucket. The telephone rang. Gus honked.

'Hullo, hullo, I can't hear you.'

'This is Piers.'

'Yes, John, how are you?'

'Haven't you had your phone mended yet?'

'No.'

'You should. It's months since that dog bit it, broke it.'

'What?'

'I said it's months since –'

'He hated the bell, the noise hurt his ears, so he jumped at it, bit it.'

'You should get it mended, it won't cost you anything.'

'Oh.' Matilda ran a finger over the sellotape holding the machine together.

'He's dead anyway.'

'I can't hear you.' She smiled at Gus in the doorway shifting from foot to foot.

'I said he's dead.'

'I heard you. What do you want?'

'I want to know how you are.'

'I'm all right, John.'

'Piers.'

'All right, Piers. It's awfully silly to change your name at your age.'

'It's always been Piers.'

'John to me. This call's costing you a lot. What do you want?'

'Are you coming to London?'

'Don't know.'

6

'Do you good to have a change.'

'I'm going to have one.'

'Going somewhere nice?'

'I can't hear you.'

'Get the phone mended.'

'What?' She waved to Gus.

'Heard from the children?'

'Yes, no, fairly lately.'

'Matilda.'

'Yes?'

'Get the phone mended, it's dangerous, you might need it urgently.'

'Mind own biz.'

'What?'

'Goodbye, John.'

'Piers.'

'All right, Piers.' She replaced the receiver, lifted the bucket out of the sink and sloshed water over the table stained by similar previous events. The wet wood steamed in the sun.

'Like some maize?' She stood looking down at Gus. 'Come on then.' Gus followed her while she fetched the maize. She threw a little on the grass. The gander ignored it.

'Gus, you must eat.' She sat down and the bird climbed onto her lap. 'Eat, you fool.' She held the bowl. Gus ate a little, pushing the corn about with his beak while she stroked him, pressing her hand along his back then curving it round his breast. 'You must keep up your strength for all those pretty ladies. You will like them, you know you will. You won't be lonely with them.'

Gus got off her lap to stroll about cropping grass before coming back to stand behind her, leaning his neck over her shoulder, twisting it to peer up into her eyes.

Matilda sat looking down the valley, tired, trying to think whether there was anything left undone.

The house was scrubbed, polished, hoovered, the beds made up with the best linen. Silver, brass and copper shining. Stores in the cupboards and larder. Bills paid, desk tidy, list of the whereabouts of people and things they would need all written, every spider captured and put outside before its web was destroyed. All done. Only the picnic basket and bathing things to get now. And Gus.

'Such a betrayal. I can't help it, Gus. Geese can live to be thirty or more. I can't wait. You will be all right.'

A landrover drove up the lane, stopped by the gate. A man got out. Matilda stood. Gus honked angrily, the rims of his eyes showing red. Matilda shook hands while Gus hissed and threatened the man's ankles, his neck stretched out, head low.

'Good afternoon. He's a fine bird. I brought a sack.'

'Oh yes, you said. You said that would be the best way. Would you like a drink?'

'No thank you, I'd better not. If I get this fellow loaded up I'll be on my way, then he'll have time to get to know his harem before dark.'

'They won't hurt him?'

'No, no, no, a gander rules his geese. They haven't heard of women's lib.'

'He rules me –' The man nodded, unsmiling, looking down at Gus.

'Your other gander?' She glanced away.

'A fox got him. I think I told you.'

'Yes, of course you did.'

'Gus, don't!' The man sidestepped as Gus pecked his calf. 'I'm so sorry.'

'That's all right. Thick trousers. I keep them all shut up at night now. He'll be safe.'

'He's always slept in the scullery.'

'Well yes, but he will get used to his shed, stable actually, stone floors, geese are messy birds. I hose them down, the stables.'

'I slosh water over the scullery floor, it's got a drain in the middle, a sort of grating.' What a stupid conversation. Couldn't he get on with it and go? 'Shall we get him into the sack?'

'Okay. You pick him up as you know him, put him in.

8

That's right. I'll tie this round his neck so that he can't hurt himself Ouch! That was sharp.'

'He's frightened.'

'Yes, of course. There we are. I'll take him now, he'll be all right, don't worry. Soon he'll be with his harem. Six of them.'

The man carried Gus to the landrover, put him over the tailboard. Gus did not stop honking as the man drove away.

'Fucking harem. I must be mad.' Matilda went indoors, poured herself a stiff whisky, switched on the radio for the weather report. High pressure continuing over the Atlantic, very hot, very dry.

The telephone began to peal again. Matilda went up to the instrument and pulled off a strip of cellophane, letting it ring until it tired. Now the picnic. She took a basket and put in butter, rolls, a slab of rather runny Brie, some peaches, a knife, a corkscrew, a bottle of Beaujolais.

'Right,' she said out loud. 'Right, I'm ready then.' A final look round the house, appallingly clean, strange. She shut the windows and the front door, picked up the basket. A spider of vast size scurried in at the kitchen door across the floor and under the dresser. 'You win.' Matilda stepped out carrying the basket, locked the door, put the key under the bootscraper where only a fool would leave it for any fool to find. Into the garage, into the car, start it up, drive off. 'If you exist keep an eye on Gus. See that he is all right. Please.' Matilda prayed without faith as she drove fast down the lane which led to the main road. A god with wings was a credible God but not in the guise of a man driving a landrover. Matilda trod hard on the accelerator. The noise of the engine failed to drown the sound in her mind of betrayed honking.

In the empty house the telephone rang to an audience of one spider.

2

She switched on the car radio to drown the sound in her mind. I will not think of it. I will suppress it, forget it, bury it as I have done with other things all my life. Go away Gus, go away. She turned up the sound.

For many days now she had carried her transistor about the house and listened as she scrubbed, swept, hoovered, polished, dusted. As she worked she had heard Mozart, Beethoven, Bach and Brahms, pop and pop and pop, the news. Rumours of war, violence, here, there and everywhere, only it isn't war now, she had thought, it is Guerillas, often pronounced Gorillas, who bomb, shoot or kidnap, hijack planes and trains. An active lot these Guerillas/Gorillas, forever in the news, by no means unsympathetic, full of ideals and always on the hour every hour between quiz games or music, *Woman's Hour, Listen with Mother.* the news and weather imperceptibly changing as the days passed and she startled spiders, catching them in a tumbler, putting them out of doors before destroying their webs. The weather hot, continuing hot, traffic jams on the motorways, the French industrialist kidnapped from his home, the vanished bride on her honeymoon – perhaps she had realized her error, fled – and the Matricide. The police hunt for the Matricide and the Vanished Bride followed her upstairs and down as she dusted and swept, lifting the transistor from one piece of furniture to the next.

She had considered matricide. Why was killing your mother so special? Worse than killing your wife? Your child? Worse than being a Guerilla/ Gorilla? He looked

10

quite nice in the photo they showed on the box. Six foot two, they said, brown eyes, fair hair, large nose, speaks with an educated accent. One would hope so from a person who had weathered Winchester, Cambridge and the Sorbonne. One would hope so but just as able to kill his mother as the Guerillas were able to blow people up, shoot them down. A lot of Guerillas had also been to the Sorbonne or Harvard or Oxbridge.

Matilda had thought, as she put clean sheets on the beds, that anyone with any gumption was capable of anything if brave or annoyed enough. She, when she had a mother, had often longed to kill her to stop the incessant prying and interfering, the possessiveness. Poor Matricide she had thought vaguely, her mind turning to her own children. Did they? Would they? They would like to, she decided, noticing that there was now a talk on roses purring out of the radio. They would like to but they were not among the brave – possibly Claud. Yes, Claud –

He had, this Matricide, killed his mother with a tea-tray. Marvellous! A heavy silver tea-tray. How nice to be rich. Had he when a child toboganned down the stairs on a tea-tray? Perhaps people who went to these posh educational establishments didn't.

The spiders were a great worry. Old cottages were full of spiders of all sizes, some as large as a mouse when they scurried across the floor at night, others tiny, found in the mornings in the bath with wistful legs. Anyway, it being August and the Silly Season, the media babbled on about the Matricide every day, though it was true not quite so much latterly, rather favouring the Bride. He had not been seen since he left his mother's house after banging her on the head with the tray, not been seen so not been caught.

'Makes the police look silly,' Matilda had said to Gus feeding him his midday mush. 'Makes the police look idiotic, doesn't it?' Gus had made his throttling noises and Matilda had gone back to sweeping away her house's character. 'Dirt of ages,' she had hummed to a

11

religious programme. 'Dirt of ages made by me! Oh, how filthy I do be.' Well, it was all clean and tidy now, Matilda thought, as she drove, and although it's latish, not sunset yet. Not quite yet, time enough for my picnic. I have tidied myself out of my house with the spiders. I betrayed Gus. Now I can have my picnic in peace, delicious Brie and Beaujolais unbothered by God in trousers. Petrol. It would be stupid to run out of petrol. She drew in at a garage and waited. No attendant came.

'It's self-service,' a man called to her, easing himself into the driving seat of his car and adjusting the safety belt across his stomach.

'Oh hell!' Matilda felt shame. 'Bloody hell!' She got out of the car flushing with hate.

'Excuse me, could you – I can never manage, would you fill her up for me, please?'

The man there to take cash, give change, watch that there was no hanky panky came slowly out of his glass box. He exuded contempt, the chauvinist swine.

'How many?'

'Fill her up, please.' Matilda waited by the glass box watching the man jiggle with the petrol pump, push the nozzle roughly into the tank, stand idly as the liquid gurgled in. Sexy in a dreary way, she thought. Inside the glass box the man's radio was playing. 'Here is the news.' She listened to the weather, still fine and hot. The Prime Minister – the Common Market – the airport strike – the bomb alert – the hijack in Italy – the kidnapping in France – the five sightings of the Matricide seen in Los Angeles, Hong Kong, Bermondsey, Brighton and Kampala. High pressure over the Atlantic would continue for some days –

'Any news?' The man came back.

'Only the usual stuff. What do I owe you?'

The man named the price. Matilda paid exactly counting out the change, which seemed to irritate the man.

'Sorry. I thought it would help.'

'Ah, you remind me of my mother, she's pernickety too.'

12

Matilda felt insulted. There was something bourgeois about being pernickety.

'Do you want to murder her?'

'Sometimes.' The man laughed. 'Only sometimes.' He was counting the money. 'Guess he did away with himself. Here, you gave me 10p too much. Got remorse poor sod.'

'Oh, sorry.'

'Your loss not mine.'

'Not quite as pernickety as you thought.'

'No.' The man grinned. 'Did they say what ransom those French kidnappers are asking?'

'I didn't hear. I don't think it said. Why?'

'Good way to make a packet.'

'Yes, I suppose so. Well, goodbye. Thank you.' Matilda got back into her car, leaving the safety straps unused. They hung dusty and twisted. She was afraid of them, afraid of being tied down, tied in. She checked that her picnic basket and bag were safe – bathing suit, lipstick, comb, pills for hayfever, pills.

'The Pillage'. Rather a bad pun but it had been funny in the context he had used it in. 'Now then,' Matilda muttered, starting the engine, 'don't think of *him*, don't think of Stub and don't think of Prissy, think of anything else, Gus, no, not Gus. That fat man tying himself in so carefully. Did he feel loved and wanted? For crying out loud, how could he be wanted, so fat and ugly?' She drove fast but carefully, not wanting an accident. The radio was playing pop. She turned it off and began to sing:

'Pop, pop, poppity pop
They all pop in and
They all pop out
Pop is the name of the girl inside
She sells the ginger pop you see!'

Why had her grandmother told her not to sing it? Was it vulgar or was there some hidden indecent Edwardian meaning? What silly things she remembered from childhood. She went on singing. 'Pop, pop, poppity pop. Must pay attention here, not miss the turning' – which led by devious lanes to the cliffs from where she would walk to the beach.

'They all pop in and –' here was the turning, a lot of cars waiting to get out onto the main road, people hot and sunburned, tired after too long a day on the beach, on their way home to supper, tea or the pub.

As she swung the car into the lane she caught the eyes of a holiday dog hanging his head out of a car window.

'They all pop out
Pop is the name of the girl inside
She sells the ginger *pop* you see!'

Matilda didn't want to think about dogs. Suddenly she realized why her grandmother did not like her to sing the ditty. Miss Renouff, blue eyes and shingled hair, had taught it to her. Grandpa had cast-an appraising eye in that direction. All dead now of course. All popping over for that lot.

The lane twisting between tall banks led to the cliffs. She parked the car in the cliff car park, took out her picnic basket, swung her bag over her shoulder, locked the car.

All round her families with children were packing into their cars, getting ready to leave. Matilda picked her way past waste paper, lolly sticks, torn cellophane and remains of picnics, tipped – but not into the wire baskets provided. She wondered whether to pause, collect a few Coca Cola tins and beer cans and put them into the basket, but the jibe 'pernickety' still rankled. She kicked a can with her espadrille and watched it merrily roll.

All the way along the cliff path she met weary holiday-makers returning.

'Pop, pop, poppity pop, I shall have the beach to myself,' she hummed, strolling neither fast nor slow, carrying the basket with the Brie, the rolls, the peaches and the Beaujolais swinging along downwards, twisting and turning down from the top of the tall granite cliffs to

14

the beach and the sea sighing gently over the sand to stroke the line of pebbles until they rattled. The tide was up, would soon turn and drag itself out across the sand leaving it clean and smooth for her feet.

Matilda paused at the bottom of the cliff path. Three lots of people were getting ready for the long climb up. One group was having a last swim. Matilda had seen them before, knew their routine. They would soon be gone. She walked along the stones enjoying her rope soles. At the far end of the beach she stopped by the favourite rock. Here she would sit in the sun and wait. She put the basket in the shade and undressed, pulling on the bathing suit, deciding to swim before the picnic. It was early yet. It would be light for a long time.

Out to sea a boat sailed slowly across the bay. She could hear the voices of the people on board and a dog barking. The boat had a blue sail.

Not wanting to wet her hair she walked into the sea and swam slowly, breast stroke, no effort, her body received by the wonderfully warm sea. Here so often they had swum, paddling out slowly and chatting with the same closeness as the closeness of bed but unleavened by sex. Matilda, swimming gently, savoured the memory of long swims, the easy talk, the intimacy, remembering conversations wrapped in water, their heads close, bodies floating. A long way out she turned to look at the cliffs which were so like Sounion.

Down the zigzag track came a party of people, young, lithe, noisy. They laughed and talked among themselves. They carried armfuls of rugs, carrier bags, spare sweaters. In jeans and T-shirts they were beautiful and young. Two girls danced down the track swinging a bottle of wine in each hand. Their voices carried across the water.

'Bobby and Vanessa collect the driftwood. We'll get the fire for the barbecue going while you swim.'

'Super, it's so warm we can sleep down here.'

'Super, super.'

'I shan't sleep, I shall watch the moon. Super.'

15

'I shall watch Vanessa.'

'Super.'

'Let's swim naked.'

'Super.'

'Not yet, there's someone in the water.'

'Oh, bugger, is there?'

'Yes, but she'll soon be gone.'

'Oh yes. Oh, isn't it super.'

Cold, sick with disappointment Matilda swam for the shore, thrusting her arms through the unwelcome sea no longer hers.

Slowly, bitterly she dried herself. The barbecue party had settled fifty yards away. Fifty yards and the beach was half a mile long.

'I'd meant to use that flat rock she's on as a table but she's on it. It's got useful dips which hold the food. I mix the salad in one of them.'

'She'll be gone soon, don't worry. It's a super rock, just the job, super.'

Matilda slowly rubbed her legs, pushing the towel down to her ankles, up, then down again.

'I thought we'd have it to ourselves, it's always empty at this time, everyone goes home,' the boy arranging the fire grumbled.

'We will. It's super. She won't be long, she's drying herself, look.'

Matilda rubbed her arms, looking out to sea where the boat with the dog on board sailed slowly, the sail turning purple. The barbecue party moved continuously, bringing driftwood, fidgeting, throwing their long young limbs about. Their inane voices carried in the clear air.

'Shall we swim now or later?'

'I want to swim naked.'

'Super! Why not?'

'Well –'

'She'd go more quickly if we stripped.'

'Super. Do strip Bobby – go on.'

Matilda pulled off her bathing suit and dried herself standing on the hot rock, baked all day in the sun.

16

'Christ! She's stripped. D'you think she heard us?'

'No, of course not. She's old, she can't have.'

'Old people aren't necessarily deaf.' The girl called Vanessa spoke crisply.

'Oh Vanessa, you are so witty, why don't you strip?'

'I'm not beautiful enough or old enough not to care.'

She meant me to hear that, Matilda thought, sitting down on the warm rock. That girl would murder her mother without hesitation if she thought she wouldn't be caught. There's no passion in that voice. I bet the Matricide has passion.

'I want that flat rock as a table. I had it all planned.' The voice held a whining note.

'She'll be gone soon.'

'Yes, poor old bird.'

Feeling the rock warm on her bottom Matilda reached for her shirt thinking. 'Yes, I'll be gone soon, you despoilers of my beach.'

Pulling her shirt on and buttoning it slowly she suddenly wept, remembering this rock with – well, with him her love, he lying back, his hips in one of the hollows, his crane-like legs stretched long and thin towards the sea, grey hair falling back onto the rock, the colour of the granite and the hair merging. Or of watching him stepping slowly along the edge of the water like a heron, unhurried, thoughtful, beaky nose, grey hair, elongated legs, flapping his arms to tease Stub who barked to attract his attention, to make him play, and the children tailing heel and toe along the sand, pressing in toes to form a pattern with Stub's paw marks, Stub who dearly loved swimming and even once with Gus who had become so emotional he'd messed all over the rock and the car going home. Matilda let herself pee allowing the hot urine to flow into a dip in the rock. She stood up, dried between her legs, pulled on her jeans, zipped them.

'She isn't wearing knickers,' a girl's voice hissed. 'Fancy, an old person like that!'

Matilda picked up her bag and slung it over her

shoulder. She remembered she had a sweater in the car and was glad. She took up her basket feeling the weight of the Beaujolais. It would be heavier by the time she got back to the car park.

'Goodnight – there's your table.' she said, moving off away from the barbecue party and the rock gently steaming.

'Oh. Goodnight. Thanks. Super.'

'Have a good time.'

'Thanks, we will.'

'Do you think she was listening to us?'

'Of course she was, the old bitch.'

Matilda grinned, walking barefoot along the sand.

3

A long haul up the goat track. That voice – 'one more twist, one more turn – nearly there, nearly there now.' Voices linger in the mind long after the face blurs. The muscles of her thighs hurt as they always did. Her breath came short, her heart beat. A matter of honour not to stop, however slow one went, until the top. She remembered another very steep path at Le Brusc down to the pebbles in the cove, no sand there, and the hair-raising climb at Pedney Founder where they hauled themselves up clutching at clumps of thrift.

What madness to bring Gus here. Still, he had adored the sea even if he had hissed and honked all the way up the cliff. Stub had barked running ahead and then run back to encourage them. The top at last. Matilda set down the heavy basket, dropped her bag and sat gasping, her legs trembling. Away on the horizon the boat sailed almost out of sight, below on the beach the young people had the fire going, the food laid on the flat rock. Two girls were swimming in water as clear here as in Greece, their hair streaming behind them. They were naked. Their distant voices cried 'Super! Oh, it's super!' Super for some. Would he lay the salad on the rock and would a girl cry, 'Oh Bobby, what a super salad dressing. What did you put in it? I've never tasted anything like it, it's super.'

Her heart steadied, her breathing slowed. Matilda looked at the view. She was humming a Brandenburg Concerto now. Away to the west were other beaches but all with easy access and car parks. What to do?

Back to the car.

She shouldered her bag, picked up the basket, walked along the cliff, strolling slowly. There was heaps of time. The tide must go out, pause, and come in again. She had to fill in time. That was all. A little more waiting didn't matter. The car smelt of hot metal. Matilda opened the windows, started the engine and drove slowly to the town down the steep streets to the harbour car park. With difficulty she found a place. She locked the picnic basket in the car and set off to wander round.

The town wore its summer face: shops with souvenirs, striped awnings, clusters of buckets, spades, beach balls, racks of picture postcards, the harbour full, every mooring filled. Now was the time for yachtsmen to come ashore, drink long, talk loudly in the pubs, boring on in yard-arm voices. Matilda strolled slowly among the people, observing the fat women in tight trousers or bikinis. They did not seem to mind their bulges burned red by the sun. Nor did the men, their shorts held up by tight belts biting into beer stomachs, mind their shape.

The fat and middle-aged were predominant by the harbour, wandering along with peeling noses, thighs sore from rubbing together. She turned up the main street, glancing in at the shop windows. A group of people stood staring at a television shop. The colour sets were showing the news on BBC and ITV.

'I wonder what he's saying?' A small child holding his mother's hand tugged. 'Come on Mum, I'm tired.'

'Just a minute love, let's see the news.'

'You can't hear it –'

'I like that girl announcer, she's lovely.'

'I like the man best.'

'Oh look dad, that must be the Matricide.' A teenage girl in shorts pointed. 'He doesn't look like a murderer.'

'Murdered his mother, a right bastard.'

'Oh Mum, I'm tired. Can't we go home?'

'Wait a minute. There may be a new photo.'

'They've shown the same photo ever since he did it. You'd think a bloke like that would have lots of photos done.'

'I like the way she does her hair. D'you think that way would suit me, Mum?' the girl questioned.

'Ask your Dad, dear.'

'I'm tired,' whined the small boy.

'I expect with all that money he's had a nose job done by now.'

'A nose job?'

'Well anyone would recognize that great hooter.'

'Oh.' Mum sounded pleased with the idea. 'You're clever, Dad.' Dad looked gratified.

'Big hooter like that stands out a mile, don't it? So he has a nose job sharpish. That's what I read in the paper anyway, either a nose job or he's done away with himself.'

'If he had any decent feelings he'd have done that.'

'Oh Mum, I'm tired –'

'Come on, son, I'll give you a ride.' The father hoisted the little boy onto his shoulder. 'Up you go!'

'Oh look, look, they're shooting! Wait a minute, wait.' The child craned down from his father's shoulders to watch a scene of violence, bodies falling, ragged men lying legs astraddle firing guns. 'Oh look, that one's dead.' He sounded joyful. 'Look at the blood.'

'So's the Matricide's Ma.' The father started up the street carrying the boy who looked back towards the silent television, craning his neck to see death happening.

'D'you think our Mr Antoine could do my hair like that, Mum?' the girl urged.

'Don't see why not, dear. You ask him when we get home. He'll charge, mind.'

'Oh I don't mind.'

Matilda stood idly watching the man talking and pointing to the weather chart which had circles all over it in which were written 'High'. Up the street she heard the husband say to his wife, 'Bring back hanging, that's what they ought to do.'

'Hanging isn't good enough, Dad.'

'Got to catch him first, haven't they? Shouldn't be difficult with that great hooter.'

Matilda turned back down the street remembering a

pub which was relatively quiet. She would sit there and rest.

At a corner shop she bought a paper and strolled along entertaining speculations of that tired child grown up murdering his dreary mother at some future date. Why not? Children like that, perfectly commonplace children, became Guerillas and shot people.

Finding the pub with an unoccupied seat outside she ordered a whisky, sat down to wait and read her paper.

The paper was not one she was used to. She read an article on fashion, another on diet, an account of a footballer's divorce, several accounts of rail, motor and plane crashes, a new earth tremor in Guatemala. On the last page but one the usual photograph of the Matricide, now supposed to have reached Japan. He did not, Matilda thought, seem to have such a very huge nose, nothing out of the ordinary, not much larger than Tom's. The photograph could be anybody. She sipped her whisky, looked at her watch. Still early. A lot of people about, a lot of time to creep by.

Poor man. She looked at the photograph. The country was full of large noses, large cocks too. 'My God, I feel tired,' Matilda muttered, not even hungry, too tired to eat. What frightful waste of Brie. Mustn't get drunk, she thought, but one more whisky won't hurt me.

She took her empty glass to the bar. As she waited to be served she observed the people sitting round the tables or standing talking. She listened to the topics of conversation. A group of three men and a pretty girl were discussing a couple called Jeffrey and Sally. Sally had upped and left Jeffrey and gone to Ibiza with Johnnie, whose wife Vanessa had moved in with Chris.

'Which Vanessa?' asked one of the men.

'The dark one, you know her, the one they call the Dark Filly.'

Everybody laughed and chorused, 'Oh, that Vanessa,' understandingly.

'But what about Sally when she comes back?'

'She hasn't a leg to stand on. She's been having it off

22

with Charles for a year, everybody knows that.'

'But Chris doesn't.'

'No, Chris doesn't.'

'They only mind about the money. There aren't any kids.'

Gossip, thought Matilda, paying for her whisky, never varied much. She edged back to the door, noting three conversations about sailing, two about cars, another husband and wife complex. Nobody, she thought as she regained her place outside, was talking about plane, train or car crashes, terrorists, Guerillas or Earthquakes. They were so saturated with horrors they were immune to catastrophe.

Her watch said 8.30. Time creeping on. She put her whisky on the table, not wanting it now, and sat with her legs stretched out watching the passers-by.

On the whole, she reflected, the human race was unbeautiful although some of the girls in long skirts, were lovely as they passed, holding their lovers' hands, looking up into the ordinary faces of their men who, whether their noses were large, snub or crooked, were transformed by the girls' love to beauty. Matilda remembered Gus's beak and sighed. 'A great hooter.' She wondered how he was faring among the strange geese and took a sorrowful sip of whisky.

Stub's nose had been long, sad, black, Prissy's a tender pink. Matilda allowed her thoughts a brief recollection of those companions, very brief, for to think of Stub and Prissy made her think of Tom. There, the thought was there. Tom, Tom, Tom, she said in her mind. Tom, Stub, Prissy, all dead. She had said it to herself. Dead, dead, dead, those three and Gus she had betrayed. Matilda had another sip of whisky and looked down towards the harbour.

I am a great betrayer, she thought. That is my sin. I am not a sticker. I betray from laziness, fear and lack of interest.

Beyond the harbour the sea was growing dark, on board the boats were lights and laughter. The sailors had returned from the pubs to cook their suppers.

Matilda stood up, leaving her whisky unfinished, pulled her bag over her shoulder. Inside the bar the musak was turned up and with it rose the decibels of conversation as she started down the street. The voices cried, 'Ignition', 'It's only the money!', 'If we altered the spinnaker', 'I really think a Jag is best never mind the Japanese'. Matilda went down to the harbour.

She reached the bridge where the river joined the sea. Peering over the parapet she could see that the tide was up, about to turn. A feeling of intense excitement almost made her cry out. She gripped the parapet, stared down at the water, secret, black; soon with the tide running out there would be ripples, as sweet flowed into salt to be drawn out to sea, swing west with the current far beyond the cliffs, round the bay a long way out under the sickle moon.

Suddenly she felt furiously hungry.

She looked at her watch, luminous in the dark. Too late. She felt cheated.

'No Brie, no rolls, no Beaujolais. Damn', muttered Matilda, 'Damn and blast!'

She only realized she had spoken aloud when a man, also leaning over the parapet, shifted his feet. She felt fury. What business had he here, how dare he invade her privacy?

Would he go away? He must. There was nothing to keep him here unless, she thought with a sinking heart, he has a tryst. He is meeting his girl. Curse him, she thought. Curse him and his girl. She looked at him sidelong, not turning her head. He looked dreadfully tired. He couldn't be meeting a girl as tired as that. He leant on his elbows, his face in his hands, obviously exhausted. A car passed, driving slowly across the bridge, heading away to the country beyond the town. The man did not move or look up. Perhaps he was drunk. Matilda risked a quick glance. Tall but slumped with depression.

Oh God! Matilda thought to herself, he's going to throw himself over! The selfish brute, he bloody well mustn't. I shall just stay until he goes. She willed him to move, to leave, to push off.

A boy and girl came walking so closely entwined they nearly tripped each other up. They stopped in the middle of the road to kiss, their bodies clenched. Matilda, exasperated, willed them to move on but they continued kissing.

The man paid no attention, leaning lost in thought on the parapet.

Perhaps he's drugged, Matilda thought.

A police car came crawling slowly. The driver gave a little toot. The boy and girl looked up, faces dazed with love.

'Oh piss off,' called the girl, moving to one side out of the boy's arms. 'Piss off,' she yelled.

The constable beside the driver wound down his window. 'Now then Brenda, now then –'

'Piss off.'

'I'll tell your dad,' called the constable. The driver laughed.

The boy lifted two fingers. 'Come on,' he said to the girl. 'Bloody fuzz.'

'Fucking public here. Come on then, Eddy.' The girl retwined herself round the boy. They moved awkwardly away.

Matilda's heart beat in heavy thumps. She moved along the parapet closer to the man. Two yards from him she said in a low voice, apologetic:

'I'm dreadfully sorry but I saw your face in the lights of the police car.'

'Yes?'

'They'll be coming back.'

'I daresay they will.'

'Well, I recognized you –'

'Yes.'

'Are you going to throw yourself over?'

'It had occurred to me.'

'Well, are you or aren't you?'

'I haven't made up my mind.'

25

'Oh.'

'I was undecided.'

'Well, I wasn't. I'm just waiting for the tide to be right. You are rather –'

'De trop?'

'Yes.'

The Matricide laughed, leaning against the parapet. 'So sorry.' He choked with laughter. 'So sorry to be in your way. I'll move if you like.'

'Put your arm round me. The police car's coming back. Quick.' The Matricide put his arm round her shoulders.

'Round my waist, you fool. My hair is white but it looks fair in this light.' Matilda pressed her face against him. 'I look young in the dark.'

The police car crawled by, the constable talking on the car radio. 'No, nothing Sarge. Willco. Roger. Out.'

'They do dearly love their radio.' He bent back a little. 'You haven't shaved.'

'Haven't since –'

'Well, I think that's silly. The first thing they expect is for you to grow a beard and have plastic surgery to your nose.'

'D'you realize I killed my mother?' he said gently.

'Of course. Lots of people long to. You just did it.'

'Oh.'

'Oh hell!' exclaimed Matilda. 'I've missed the tide. Damn and blast!'

'I *am* sorry.' Sarcastic.

'Well it's too late. I can't now. You have to be exact about these things,' she said angrily.

'If you'd jumped –'

'Yes?'

'I would have tried to save you.'

'How ridiculous. Interfering.'

'You saved me just now.'

'That's instinctive.'

'What now? I'm in your hands. Hadn't you better take me to the police?'

26

'If that's what you want you can go by yourself. Are you hungry?'

'Starving.'

'Come on then, I've got some Brie in the car – I was going to picnic first. Brie and a bottle of Beaujolais.'

'Sounds tempting.'

'Put your arm round me and your head against mine.'

'I'm rather too tall.'

'Don't make difficulties, it isn't far.' They walked in a loverly way to the car park.

4

Matilda unlocked the car. 'Get in,' she said. 'I'll get the food.' She reached for the basket on the back seat. 'Could you uncork this?' She handed him the bottle and corkscrew.

'I think so.' In the dark he fumbled, holding the bottle between his knees. Matilda buttered a roll and spread the Brie. The cork popped.

'Go ahead and drink. I haven't a glass. I wasn't bothering for myself –'

'But –'

'Go on, take a swig. I'm all right, I've been drinking whisky, waiting for the tide to turn, for it to get dark.'

He drank, tipping up the bottle. Matilda watched his profile. Not such a very large nose after all.

'The way the papers write about your nose you might be Pinocchio.'

'That was marvellous.' He handed Matilda the bottle and took the roll. 'Thank you.'

Matilda watched him eat. After cramming in half a roll he ate slowly.

'There's some salad and a peach. Cyrano de Bergerac too.'

'Really?' He sounded amused.

'Yes, really.'

'What's your name?'

'Matilda Poliport.'

'Married?'

'Widow.'

'Sorry – sad.'

'One gets used to it. No, that's not true, one never does.'

'My name is Hugh Warner.'

'I'm glad to know it. I must have heard or read it but for two weeks you've just been the Matricide on the radio and television. Have another roll? Your photo's in all the papers.'

'Thank you.' He took another roll. 'That your dog? Surely you were not going to leave her behind?'

Matilda looked down. Looking into the car a canine face, paws just reaching the car window.

'Not mine. I have no dog.'

'She looks dreadfully hungry.' He held out half his roll. The dog snapped at it, gulped, retreated a few paces.

'Now you've done it.'

'Done what?'

'Got yourself a dog. Can't you see she's lost? Look how thin she is. If you looked at her paws you'd see they are sore. That's a lost dog.'

'We can take it to the police when you take me.'

'I'm not taking you, you can manage by yourself.'

'Look pretty silly if I walk in and say "Hi, Constable, I'm the Matricide and here's a lost dog, will you arrest us." '

They began to laugh quietly at first then in great whoops. Tears trickled down Matilda's cheeks. She watched him feed the last roll to the dog, bit by bit, luring her into the car until she sat on his knee and licked his face.

'Look at her paws. Poor little thing, oh poor little thing.' The dog licked Matilda's face also.

'Well?'

'Well?'

'I'm still frightfully hungry. Will the police feed me, d'you think?'

'Not for hours. They ask questions first.'

'Oh dear,' he sighed, stroking the dog, tipping up the bottle for another drink. 'That was delicious.'

'Any left for me?'

He handed her the bottle. She drank, tipping it up three quarters empty, her eyes looking over to the black water in the harbour reflecting the lights from the town. She finished the bottle and reached back to put it in the basket.

'Here's a peach.' He ate. The dog watched him.

'You wouldn't like fruit.' His hand fondled the dog's tatty ears. 'She's a frightful mongrel,' his voice tender.

Matilda wiped her face with her handkerchief, tidied up the remains of the picnic. 'She's lost and unwanted. I think we can skip the police.'

'Ah. You are soft.'

'Absolutely –' Matilda began to speak then stopped, remembering Gus. 'No, I'm not soft. I don't know what I am. I hate. I hate. I'm full of it.'

'Pretty soft sort of hate.'

'It would be difficult to resist, just look at her.' The dog now lolled between them, her body relaxed, sore paws hanging down, small black eyes moving from one face to the other.

Matilda tried to think. She had failed to carry out the planned picnic. 'I've missed the tide,' she mewed.

'You can try tomorrow.'

'Not with this dog and –'

'And?'

'All that planning gone to waste.'

'Carefully worked out, was it?'

'Yes.'

'So sorry.'

'No good being sorry,' Matilda said briskly. 'No good us just sitting here.' She switched on the engine. 'I daresay you'd like a bath.'

'A bath would be thrilling. They have them in the nick I understand.'

Matilda switched on the headlights, drove out of the car park up through the town. Her passenger did not speak.

On the outskirts of the town Matilda saw a corner shop still open. She stopped the car. 'Won't be a minute.'

She got out, went into the shop and bought several large cans of dog food, two pints of milk, a carton of eggs. 'When I get back to the car he will be gone,' she thought. 'Perhaps he will take the dog. It would be an intelligent thing to do; nobody is looking for a man with a dog. If he's gone I shall go straight back to the cliffs and whether that barbecue is going on or not, I shall swallow my pills and swim out, though washed down with milk isn't as fine as washed down with Beaujolais, but if I swim fast the pills will work on their own. My plan will work after all.'

She took the carrier bag back to the car. Hugh Warner was fast asleep holding the dog in his arms. Matilda restarted the car. She sensed her passenger was awake though he did not speak.

They drove out of the town past the bus station, the railway station and the police station. Matilda grinned to herself momentarily, forgetting her resolution.

'It's about ten miles.'

'I see.'

'You can have a bath and go to bed or you can go to bed and have a bath in the morning. There's food in the house.'

'I'd love a bath.'

'Okay.'

'If you have a razor?'

'Yes.'

'A bath and a shave, how civilized. My feet are sore like Miss here. What shall you call her?'

'Folly,' said Matilda.

'A very good name.'

They drove along the main road. When she reached the turning leading to the hills she said: 'I live in an isolated cottage. It is not overlooked. I am a solitary person, people do not often come. You will be as safe as it is possible to be.'

'You are very kind.'

'I hope you appreciate my tact in not asking you why you killed your mother.'

31

'I do, immensely.'

'Good.'

'And I hope you will also appreciate my tact in not asking you why you had planned your suicide.'

'Oh I do, I do.' Matilda began to laugh again. Sitting on Hugh Warner's lap, Folly wagged her tail. Her problem at least was solved.

5

The back door key was under the bootscraper where she had left it. Matilda opened the door and, switching on the light, walked in.

'What a spotless kitchen.' Hugh, carrying the bag of food, followed with Folly at his heels.

'It's rather untidy usually.' She felt the Rayburn which was still warm, opened its door. In the fire box embers glowed. 'I expected it to be out.' She threw in sticks and a few larger pieces of wood, opened the damper. The fire flared and she put on coke. 'Could you feed Folly? Don't give her too much. The tin opener's on the wall.'

Hugh opened a tin. 'Is there a dog bowl?'

'There on the shelf.' Matilda handed him Stub's bowl. 'I bet she's thirsty.' She filled the water bowl and watched the dog drink while the man spooned out food. 'That's enough. Too much will make her sick.'

They watched the dog eat. Matilda sighed and muttered.

'What did you say?'

'I said "another hostage to fortune" – I had just got free.'

He looked at her curiously.

'If you give her a run out at the back I'll get us some food. She may not be housetrained. It's a walled garden. She won't run away.'

'What about me?' He snapped his fingers for the dog.

'You needn't run any more tonight. You can eat and sleep.'

He went out with the dog.

Matilda went upstairs to switch on the immersion heater and turn down the bed in the spare room. She opened the window and leaned out. In the oak tree up the lane an owl screeched. There was no other sound but the stream trickling over its stony bed. She felt terribly hungry. In her bedroom she opened windows and let in the warm night. The house caught its breath and came to life.

In the kitchen the man sat slumped in the beechwood chair, the dog at his feet, nose straining towards the stove. He said: 'She's a good little dog, your Folly.' The dog pricked her ears but looked at neither of them.

'She's yours, not mine. I'll get something to eat. Could you manage an omelette?'

'Lovely.'

'Salad?'

'Yes please.'

'You'll find wine in the larder. The corkscrew's in that drawer.' Matilda took a torch from the dresser and went out into the garden, shining it along the rows of vegetables, choosing a lettuce.

The sky was a mass of stars, windless. Were Vanessa and Bobby still on the beach? Had the barbecue been a success? The torch focused on a toad crawling slowly across the brick path, his eyes golden. With concentration he pulled first one long back leg up then the other. He knew his destination.

She laid the table, broke eggs, made a salad, found biscuits and butter, poured the wine, cut bread.

'It's a bit cold.'

'It doesn't matter.'

The eggs sizzled and spluttered in the pan. She cut the omelette in half and tipped it onto their plates.

They ate in silence. Matilda felt strength return slowly. Their plates empty, they sat looking at each other across the table, sizing one another up.

Matilda saw a man of thirty-five, she knew his age from the radio. Large nose, large mouth, light brown hair, not fair as the papers said, brown eyes, thick eyebrows, stubbled face drawn with fatigue, good teeth, a few definite lines.

Hugh saw a woman in her fifties, blue eyes, very white hair, arched nose, good teeth, slightly runaway chin, sensual mouth.

'You don't look like a Major.'

'They confused me with my brother; he is a Major. I expect he will be furious, bad for his image.'

'Is he fighting Guerillas?'

'He is actually. Why?'

'Such a lot of fighting. I don't approve.'

'Pacifist?'

'I just don't like violence.'

'I –'

'You hit your mother. It may have been justified.'

'What makes you think that?'

'The choice of weapon. A tea-tray. Really!' Matilda began to laugh. 'Oh dear, I'm drunk. So sorry. It's the anticlimax. I was worked up, was all prepared – I was ready.' Folly put her paws on Matilda's knees and buried her face in her crotch sniffing deeply, pressing her jaw against Matilda's thighs. She stroked the dog's head.

'Silky.'

Hugh Warner yawned.

'I'll show you where you sleep.' Matilda stood up. 'This way.'

He followed her upstairs.

'Here's your room, the loo, the bath. Sleep well.' She left him abruptly. Folly followed her back to the kitchen.

Matilda poured the last of the wine and stood drinking it, trying to think. Her head was looping the loop. With tipsy care she cleared the table, washed up, put everything away, stoked the fire once more and tipped the ashes into the bin outside the back door. Followed by the dog she went upstairs, undressed and got into bed. Without hesitation the dog got up on the bed and settled, pressing into the small of her back. Matilda thought, I shall never sleep, I'm drunk, and fell asleep instantly, her mouth open, snoring.

Along the passage Hugh Warner soaked in a boiling bath, sat up and shaved, then ran in more hot water to soak again. He washed his hair, his hands, his feet, his whole exhausted body until finally, when the water cooled, he dried himself and crawled naked into the bed assigned him and lay listening to the night sounds.

A stream somewhere near.

Owls.

Traffic a long way off.

Snores. 'Down the passage my hostess snores.' Relaxed for the first time for weeks, he smiled. What folly. He turned on his side and slept.

Half an hour later Matilda sat up in bed screaming, soaked in sweat, trembling. Folly licked her face, wagging her tail.

'He's a murderer, a murderer, he murdered his mother.' Speaking this aloud made it true. She shivered, the sweaty nightdress cooling to clamminess on her body.

'Fuck!' She tore off the nightdress and sat hugging her knees.

'Poor little dog.' Matilda stroked her. 'You will be all right now.' She switched on her bedside light to look at the time. 'Three o'clock, soon be dawn.' She lay back, pulling the sheet round her neck. The dog settled again.

If my picnic had gone according to plan I should be floating by the lighthouse. Time from now on is borrowed. The thought pleased her. She noticed from the taste in her mouth that she had been snoring, got up, rinsed her mouth with cold water at the basin then went back to lie on her side, mouth shut, breathing through her nose. How conventional to wake up and scream, how strong her upbringing. The man must have had a reason to kill his mother. Louise would, Mark could, Anabel certainly. Claud. Not Claud. Something would make him laugh or more probably he would not bother.

Time was I would have killed mine, Matilda thought, only Tom came along. It's all in the mind, she thought drowsily. It is ridiculous to scream about it. Was I not brought up not to scream? Who am I to judge? I was going to kill tonight, suicide is murder.

Hugh Warner was too deeply asleep to hear Matilda's screams. Across the British Isles the police were alert for a man answering his description. At airports and channel ports travellers' passports were examined with care. At 4 a.m. a bored journalist in Cairo filed a message that a man answering Hugh's description had been seen heading south.

Only Gus, the betrayed, shifted restless, unable to settle among the geese, utterly at a loss, anxious, disorientated, lonely.

6

Matilda thought best while occupied. Now, kneading dough, her mind came alive.

She and Folly had come down early, Folly trotting into the garden while Matilda made coffee. It was still very hot. Through the open door she could hear the hum of insects, birds singing. Away up the hill a cow cried for the calf recently taken from her. Far off a shepherd was driving sheep – she could hear the harassed bleating, the barking dogs. Folly now sat in the doorway listening.

Matilda heated up the coffee and sat at the table while the dough in its basin rose in the warmth by the Rayburn. Upstairs her visitor slept, she supposed, though he could quite easily have gone on his way while she slept. She hoped he had gone, it would be the best thing. She did not wish to be involved. Sipping coffee Matilda thought, I do not wish to get involved. Then, to be truthful: I would like to be involved and as I am why not enjoy it.

She wore a blue cotton dress, an old friend. Her legs and feet were bare, her hair still damp from washing.

About now the boat crew, probably a mackerel fisherman's, should have caught sight of her body, fished her out to bring her ashore, sent for the police and the ambulance. Matilda frowned, trying to recollect whether drowned people sank for a few days then surfaced, or floated for a few days before sinking. Not knowing bothered her. Why had she not found out this simple fact?

She divided the floury dough into four, smacked the loaves into four, pressed each with the back of a knife and put them in the oven. She would buy another bottle of Beaujolais, more butter, more Brie, another peach.

'I shall take you to the Lost Dogs Home.' Folly twitched her tail. 'But I shall have to wait for the tide to be right.' The dog wagged cheerfully. 'I do not want to grow fond of you.' The dog looked away. 'You should have gone with him. He picked you up. You are his, not mine.' Matilda listened to the silence of the cottage, certain that the man had gone. Not knowing whether the man was there or not, she felt in limbo, not wanting to readjust to living. She felt anguish choking her, cheated, for her mind had been prepared for death. She felt especially angry at the prospect of cleaning the house all over again, all those spiders.

Automatically she took the bread from the oven. If he had gone she would do as before, clean the house, weed the garden, pack her picnic, do it all again in a month. This time there would be no barbecue on the beach; the young people would have gone, their holidays over. If he had not gone she would phone the police. No, not that. They would ask questions. She would be involved. She could just imagine the questions. He would have to go off on his own before anyone saw him. She would ask him to go.

When the telephone pealed she felt fear leap in her throat. She watched the instrument as the bell jangled. Then she picked up the receiver, pinched her nose between finger and thumb and said:

'Ullo?'

'Can I speak to Mrs Poliport, please?' John's voice, crisp and terse.

'She's not here.' Only John again.

'When will she be back?'

'She didn't say.'

'Has she gone away?'

'She may have.'

'Who is that?'

'Mrs 'Oskings.'

'Mrs Hoskings who –'

39

'I clean for Mrs Pollyput. From time to time I clean. Mrs Pollyput she don't like cleaning.'

'I daresay not.'

'Not's the word. Who shall I say called? I'll write down. You should see the spiders.'

'Piers, just Piers.'

'Like at the seaside?' Matilda, holding her nose, snorted.

'Yes, like at the seaside. Write it down, please.'

'Just a minute. I'll get a pencil – sir –' added Matilda to add credence to her role. 'Oh, here's a message from her. Shall I read it to you?'

'Yes, please do.'

' "Dear Mrs Hoskings." Pretty writing Mrs Pollyput's got, hasn't she?'

'What does she say? Read it.'

'Okay. Dear etcetera, you won't want that twice will you? No. Well it says, "gone away for a change. I'll let you know when I get back. Help yourself to anything you think might spoil from the garden." '

'Is that all?'

'Yes, that's all Mr Pier. D'you think she'd mind if I took the raspberries, the birds will get them else. Shall I –'

John rang off. Matilda released her nose and sniffed, wriggling it up and down like a rabbit. Piers. How ludicrous John calling himself Piers. Piers rang a distant bell far back in her mind. Piers? No, it meant nothing, recalled nothing, it couldn't. Why this insistence on Piers? Sir John sounded all right. Claud said it was snobbery, that John was a common name. Claud had bet Anabel ten pounds John would be elevated in the Birthday List, not the New Year's, it being the more recherché of the two to enter the lists as Sir Piers in June rather than hustle in in the New Year when everyone was too hung over to notice. Not that he will allow anyone to fail to notice. 'He will never get further than a knighthood in his occupation. Decorous recognition for services rendered. No life peerage for the likes of he.' Claud's voice in her mind, always that note of affection-

40

ate mockery to keep one at arm's length, his arm's length, Claud's. No good trying to get close to that one. A slippery character, Claud, the more lovable for his inaccessibility. Standing with one hand on the rail of the Rayburn, Matilda thought of her youngest child. No hook there to hold her, however tenuously. Why did his saying 'occupation' in that tone of voice, almost as though John –

'What a superlative smell.' Hugh stood in the doorway looking in.

'You made me jump.' Matilda pretended to jump. He grinned.

'No wonder nobody recognized you,' Matilda said. 'You don't look like your photo at all in daylight.'

'I have rested. Besides –'

'Besides what?'

'I told you that photograph is one of my brother. He really has a huge nose but now he's grown a moustache it's not so noticeable.'

'The Major?'

'Yes. There's been a mistake, a mix-up.'

'Why hasn't he said?'

'He's abroad. He may not know, he might even be loyal.'

'She was his mother too.'

'He inherits.'

'Oh.' Pause. 'Like some breakfast?'

'Please.'

'I was thinking I should call the police.'

'Shall you?'

'No.' Matilda, getting coffee, had her back to him. Neither spoke for a while. She put a loaf and butter on the table, marmalade in its pot – Cooper's.

'If it were not for your interference I should be happily dead by now.' Rage suddenly choked her, tears blinded, the hand carrying the coffee pot trembled.

'It was you who interfered with me, you silly bitch. "Put your arm round me," you said, "put it round my waist." Like a fool I did. I was going to fill my pockets

41

with stones and go into the river like Virginia Woolf.'

'You hadn't made up your mind.'

'How do you know?'

'You said so – you implied.' Matilda leaned across the table screaming at him, white with sudden fury. 'You were shilly-shallying. *I* had it all planned and you spoilt it. I could kill you.'

'Do. It will save a lot of trouble. Poke that knife into my guts, then you can push off and have your picnic, drown the dog as well –' He too was shouting, handing her the knife she had pressed on the dough.

They glared at each other with hatred. The dog whimpered.

'Are we having a row?' Hugh sat back.

'Yes. I'd forgotten what it's like. It's ages since –' Matilda pushed back her hair. 'I'd forgotten about Virginia Woolf and the stones. I must remember.'

'They would prevent you swimming very far.'

'Yes.'

'Your plan was probably best for you.'

'Was?'

Hugh glanced at the dog who wagged, placating, unsure.

'Eat your breakfast. It's ages since I had a row. Makes me feel sick, my legs are trembling.'

'Soon passes.' Hugh helped himself to marmalade. 'Delicious bread.'

Matilda stood by the stove, breathing hard, watching him eat. The kitchen clock ticked. It would need winding tomorrow.

'If anyone comes to see me go through that door into the scullery. It leads to the woodshed.'

Hugh looked up, munching.

'If you want to go further cross the garden to the copse. It's thick, nobody can see you by the stream, nobody goes in there, I don't allow it.'

Hugh's eyes were on her face.

'I don't allow fishermen or hounds in there. It's mine, private, people know.'

42

'Do they pay attention?'

'Oh yes. Gus found a boy there once and terrorized him. I tied him to a bush and left him for hours. He was scared stiff – told all his friends. It worked.'

'Sounds a bit ruthless.'

'There's a badger set in there. The boy was planning to bring his friends and bait them.'

'I see.'

'So you'd be absolutely safe in the copse.'

Hugh nodded, helping himself to more marmalade.

'Or if you're upstairs, keep from the windows and go up into the loft.'

'The loft?'

'It might be raining.'

'You think of everything.'

'I'll try.'

'Why the hell should you?'

Matilda shrugged. 'I meant to be dead by now. It doesn't matter what I do, if it's any help to you.'

Hugh looked at Matilda for a long time then said: 'You and your husband must have made a formidable pair.'

'I betrayed my husband.'

'Gus?'

'Gus? Gus is a Chinese Goose, a gander – I betrayed him too.' Matilda wept while Hugh laughed.

7

Hugh looked away from Matilda, finding her tears embarrassing. Betrayed husbands come two a penny, he thought, but a goose – that's different. The dog, sitting with her nose towards the heat of the Rayburn, glanced over her shoulder. She had bright little black eyes. She wriggled her haunches, getting closer to the warmth. He wondered where she came from, who had abandoned her.

'Have you got any money?' Matilda retrieved his attention.

'Not an awful lot. I cashed a cheque – er –'

'After killing your mother?'

'Yes.'

Matilda sniffed, whether from contempt or to stop the last tear he couldn't tell. 'I have quite a lot in London but –'

'You can't go there, the police –'

'I suppose not.'

'They will have your money.'

'No, it's hidden in a safe place.'

'You sure?'

'Yes, I have a cache.'

'I can lend you money. I can cash a cheque, overdraw if need be. I can fetch your money. I'd like to.'

'That would put you to a lot of inconvenience, danger.'

'I'd like it. It would amuse me. It would be fun.'

'Law breaking.'

'No more to me than parking on a yellow line.'

'An adventure?'

'I suppose so. Have you a passport?'

'Yes. I was going to Greece after visiting my mother. I've

44

got my passport and a bit of money. I left my bag there though.'

'How much? Count it.'

Hugh pulled his wallet from his back pocket and started counting. 'Nearly two hundred.'

'That won't get you far. How much do you have in London?'

'Two thousand in cash.'

'Well then.'

'To get it I –'

'I'll get it. I've told you. Trust me. I'll go to London. You stay here and keep hidden. I'll fix you up with food. Keep out of sight. The rest's easy.'

'I need clothes.'

'Yes, the whole world knows what you are wearing. There are some of Tom's, a few things of Mark's and Claud's which they left here.'

'Your husband's?'

'He wouldn't mind. He didn't die here, he went to stay with a friend in Paris –' she paused.

'And the friend was Death?'

'That's who it turned out to be.'

'He must have been very lonely without you.'

'Perhaps. No, no, I don't think lonely.'

'Dying on his own.'

'Don't say that, you have no right.'

'Why didn't you go too?'

'I never went to Paris with him. I had responsibilities here, things to do.'

'Such as?'

'The children, our animals.'

'I thought they were grown up.'

'They are. They weren't even here. It was –'

'What was it?'

'What right have you to catechise? What business is it of yours?'

'None. Idle curiosity, I suppose.'

'Well,' Matilda burst out. 'I don't like Paris. I never went there with him. I didn't want to put our dog and cat

45

in kennels. I just didn't want to go. If I had I would have looked after him, not let him drop dead in the street, don't you see? I know I betrayed him, of course I know. They found his pills in his hotel. If I'd been there – damn you, what right have you?' Matilda felt despairing, angry. 'I always saw that he carried his pills.'

'You saved my life. That gives me the right. Folly and I have every right. We belong to you.'

'No.'

'Yes.'

Hugh buttered another piece of bread, fished in the pot for marmalade. Matilda stood with her back to the stove watching him pour more coffee, drink.

'How do you know I won't betray you? As a good citizen I should.'

Hugh grinned. 'I don't think you belong to the W.I.'

'That's not necessarily respectable.'

'Of course it is. You don't, do you?'

'No.'

'Well then.'

Matilda sighed.

'And these children – where are they?'

'Louise is married. She lives in Paris.'

'Didn't you want to see her when your husband –'

'Not particularly. Mark is in business – he centres on Hamburg. Anabel is always on the move, I never know where she is. Claud lives in America.'

'Do they come to see you?'

'They telephone sometimes. They don't really want to speak to me or I to them. What would we say?'

'So they won't have to talk to you at your funeral?'

'That's about it.'

'So you thought you'd meet the Mutual Friend?'

'It seemed the sensible thing.'

'Sensible.' He stressed the word.

'Yes, sensible. Without Tom I've no attachment to life. The children don't want me. I was left with our dog, our cat and Gus. The dog died four months ago, the cat was caught in a gin and died of blood poisoning. Gus could

46

live another twenty years. I've found him a good safe home with geese. I've thought it all out, left everything tidy. There's nothing left for me here. I'm off.'

'But why? You can get another cat. You've got another dog.'

'That dog's yours not mine.'

'I doubt it.'

'Oh yes, she is. You picked her up. I don't want her.'

They both turned their eyes on the dog who sat with her back to them, ears laid back.

'We are embarrassing her.' Hugh snapped his fingers. The dog jumped gratefully onto his knees.

Before Hugh could speak Matilda said hurriedly:

'To people like me animals are hooks to hang one on to life. Think of the thousands of people hanging on because of the dog, the cat, the budgie. Think of all those thousands only hanging on for no other reason as they grow old, miserable, useless, bored. I bet your mother –'

'Her cat died in May. It was a smelly old thing.'

'But it didn't murder her.'

'No, there is that.'

'And she didn't replace it?'

'I tried to give her a kitten.'

'And she refused?'

'Yes, she did. She was sentimental about –'

'Old Smelly?'

'Yes. How d'you know I called it Old Smelly?'

'She didn't want to be hooked any longer, not once her company had gone.'

'I don't know.'

'No, you don't. She didn't want any more hooks. She didn't want old age, arthritis, falling down, losing her teeth, her balance, her hair, her memory, her wits. She didn't want dependence on other people, becoming a bore, growing incontinent –'

'She was very spry for her age, not at all incontinent.'

'So am I for mine, but I'm not waiting for all that: it's against my principles; creaking joints, fatigue, clicking teeth, brown spots, wrinkled bottom.'

'Bottom?'

'Of course, one wrinkles all over. I'm for the last fling – the ultimate.'

'Ultimate what?'

'Adventure. Fun. Experience.'

'That's a serious statement if you are talking about death.'

'Of course it is. I don't suppose your mother had exactly thought it all out. You saved her the trouble with your tea-tray.'

'Her tea-tray, she inherited it from her father.'

'How pedantic you are. I was starting off in good shape and got interrupted.'

'Sorry about that.' Hugh stroked Folly's ears.

'That dog is yours, as Old Smelly was your mother's.' Hugh shook his head. 'No.'

'What future had your mother?'

'There was nothing really wrong with her.'

'And nothing really right.' Matilda pounced. 'Why should you and the Major bother? You would have put her into an old people's home and forgotten her.'

'Probably.'

'That's what I can't face; losing my faculties and being put away into a safe place. I am leaving everything tidy, I'm off for my picnic, swimming out while the swimming's good. Now you've turned up and spoilt it.'

Hugh laughed. 'That's tough.'

Matilda's anger switched to merriment. 'I think you did your mother a very good turn. One good bang with a heavy tray and Whoops! she's gone. No more worries.'

Hugh winced. 'She had no worries.'

'How do you know? Sure, she had her memories. "She lives with her memories," people say. I hear them all the time. How d'you know she liked her memories? People don't necessarily like memories. Christ!' Matilda cried, 'of course they don't. Old people are like empty paper bags. You blew yours up, gave it a bang, and pop, that was the lot, her lot anyway.'

'And yours?'

48

'You've interfered.' Matilda pulled on her espadrilles. 'I'd better stop talking and go to the village, buy the papers, cash a cheque, do some shopping.'

'Very practical all of a sudden.'

'I am practical. Keep out of sight, won't you? I'll leave your dog with you. Don't answer the phone.'

'A loss to the W.I.'

'They don't think so.'

'Show me the house before you go.' Hugh stood up, towering above Matilda. 'You are the same height as my mother.'

'I don't want to think about her any more. I'll show you round.' She led the way. 'Here, in this front room if taken unawares you can hide in here or here. They are the old fireplaces, cupboards now for logs for that.' She gestured to a pot-bellied stove in the middle of the room. 'You can get right up the chimneys to the roof. Claud did once. He got filthy.' Hugh stooped and went into one of the cupboards. 'Can you stand upright? You are taller than Claud.'

'Yes.'

'Claud once locked Anabel in one and Louise in the other and went out for the day.'

'How did they get out?'

'Mr Jones heard their screams. He was passing, luckily for them. You've seen the kitchen and scullery, come upstairs. Mr Jones is my only neighbour. No bother. If you see anyone coming you can hide in those cupboards or in the one in my room, it's huge. Anyway I always know when someone is coming, Gus honks.'

'But I thought –'

'Oh God!' Matilda's eyes filled. 'I'd forgotten. How could I? He's not here, he's climbing onto all those geese, covering them, whatever it's called, or is that only for horses?'

'I don't know. I believe geese copulate.'

'I hope he enjoys it. He's had a sexually deprived life.'

'I shall keep my ears alert.'

'Yes, do that.'

'You do worry about your goose.'

'Gander. Yes I do, of course I worry. If you'd seen him in that sack driving away –'

'The cupboard upstairs.'

'Oh yes.' She led the way upstairs to the room from which he'd heard snores reverberate. 'Here's the cupboard. It's deep, it goes on for miles behind those clothes.' She pushed an open palm against hangers. 'Behind these there's lots of room. It's L-shaped, turns to the right, almost another little room.'

Hugh peered in. 'What's that?'

Matilda leant forward, her hair brushing his face. 'Ah. Claud's fancy dress.' She took a hanger off the rail and slipped a caftan over her shoulders. 'Look.' As she turned her back he saw the back of the garment was painted with a skeleton. 'He had castanets and clicked them.' She began to dance, making the skeleton move eerily. Hugh drew back in vague distaste. 'He scared the girls.'

'Why should he want to do that?'

'It was Louise, she had –' Matilda pulled the caftan round her.

'She had – what? What had she done?'

'I always think of it as the Postman's Ball. Louise was – poor Louise was going with the postman. She had planned to have him for herself. Yes, I think she had. I know she had. It was to be the postman. He wasn't the postman then. They were all at school together. It's a long time ago. I expect he's forgotten – I mean Claud – the postman wouldn't forget, one doesn't, does one?' She paused, looking at Hugh, pulling the caftan over her shoulders, putting it back on its hanger. She repeated, as she hung the caftan on the rail, 'One doesn't forget, does one?'

'Forget what?' Hugh looking down at her, thought that her skin was good for her age, smooth, hardly lined.

'One's first love. One never forgets one's first love.'

'I suppose not.'

'Claud is homosexual. The postman wasn't even pretty. I don't think he knew until Louise started making jokes, sly digs.'

50

'Not nice of her.'

'None of her business, was it?' Matilda shook her head. 'Well, behind that fancy dress there's miles of cupboard. All the garden cushions are in there for the winter. It's very clean, I've just swept it out. I've kept Claud's dress, some of Louise's and Anabel's things too. I borrow them occasionally.'

'Do they wear them when they visit you?'

'They don't visit. I have kept them in case they'd like them when I'm dead. Some of those clothes of Anabel's are dateless and Louise always buys wonderful material, she could use it to cover cushions, couldn't she?'

'Yes.'

'The boy's clothes are in your room, mixed up with Tom's. I thought –'

'What?'

'I thought I wouldn't tidy Tom away quite as much as myself. It's me they don't come and see.'

Hugh said nothing. Matilda closed the cupboard.

'If really pushed you can go up that ladder to the attic. I even cleaned that.'

'Thank you.'

'Have some more coffee before I go to the village.'

'Thanks.' Hugh followed her downstairs, noting that she walked like a dancer, straight backed.

'Are you a dancer?'

'No. I used to do yoga at one time.'

'So did my mother. She stood on her head and sat in the lotus position, all that.'

'Wasn't brisk enough to avoid that tea-tray.'

'She was frightened,' Hugh expostulated.

'I bet she was.' Matilda, reaching the kitchen, poured the coffee into a pan to reheat.

'Help yourself. I'm off.' But she lingered in the doorway, obviously wanting to say something more. Hugh looked enquiringly over the rim of his cup. 'You must think I don't love my children from the way I talk about them.'

'You seem a bit – well, casual.'

51

'They will like me better out of the way, the girls especially.'

'Why?'

'They think I love Claud best. Those dresses upstairs are dresses he pinched from them. Claud is far more beautiful than either Louise or Anabel, far more attractive.'

'You said he is gay.'

'In more ways than one.' Matilda laughed. 'He went to a party in one of those dresses in the days when boys wore their hair long. He snitched all the girls' fellows, quite disrupted Anabel's life – it was a dreadful evening.' Matilda grinned reminiscently. 'Louise had the big feller – she called him her "feller" – he went over the moon and as for Anabel's boy – well –'

'What happened?'

'Claud lives in New York.' Matilda turned on her heel and went off leaving Hugh sitting at the table, holding a cooling cup of coffee, wondering about her. With the kitchen knife in his other hand he tapped a tune on the deal table, trying to remember his actions of the last days. Then, followed by the dog, he left the house and let himself through the gate into the wood, walking along the stream until he found a patch of sunlight and sat down to watch it cunningly run and circle over the stones. Stroking the dog, who came to loll beside him, he reviewed the jumble of thoughts and terrors which had accompanied him ever since he killed his mother. They could perhaps be looked at clearly now that he had stopped running. He was puzzled that he had run at all. Why had he not stayed? Why take flight, leaving the tray flung down beside her dead body? She had looked peaceful, composed, happier than he had seen her for a long time, certainly happier than during the preceding moments when she had been in a state of extreme terror.

The extraordinary moment with the tray was clear enough, but he was still puzzled by his actions afterwards, his instant flight to his car, leaving his mother, the tray flung down beside her. She was dead. What seemed callous was that he had stopped at the bank in the town to cash as large a cheque as he could without drawing attention to himself. To be overcome by panic was unforgivable. He had driven to London, left his car in Hans Crescent then taken the Knightsbridge tube. Since then he had been on the move, expecting every minute a hand on his shoulder.

The sound of the stream was mesmeric. Hugh dozed. Matilda might not belong to the W.I. but she was capable. 'I'll go back presently and they'll be there. No more running.'

When Matilda came back with her shopping and the papers she found the cottage empty. Her feelings of relief were equal to her sense of disappointment. She was not used to ambivalence, it worried her. She looked closely in the looking glass above the sink, trying to read her feelings in her face but it was the same face as usual, a mask for whatever feelings or thoughts there might be inside this middle-aged face which was neither young nor old, neither beautiful nor ugly, just her face as usual which protected her from the prying world.

8

Matilda laid the papers on the kitchen table, put her shopping away, sat down to read. The Matricide no longer rated the front pages. No mention of him in the *Guardian*. She had not been able to buy either *The Times* or the *Daily Telegraph*, only the *Mirror*, the *Sun* and the *Express*.

'Thought you didn't read the *Express*, Mrs Poliport,' the postmaster, Mr Hicks, had remarked, taking her money.

'Fascist rag.' Matilda smiled. 'Very occasionally I like to see it, keeps the mind open to read lots of papers.'

'I read the local.'

'Yes, that tells you all you want and it's unbiased.'

'That's so.' Mr Hicks, a stout bald man, gave Matilda her change. 'Is there anything else, Mrs Poliport?' He pronounced it 'Pollyput' as did most local people.

'Oh, I nearly forgot. I need a dog licence.'

'A dog licence?' Mr Hicks had been astonished. 'I thought –'

'I know, I said never again. I know I did. I'm weak. It's a mongrel from the Lost Dogs, just a little mongrel.'

'Said you didn't want another dog, didn't want to be tied.'

'I know. I changed my mind. There it is.'

'You were offered that Boxer, pure bred.' Mr Hicks could be seen thinking even less of her than usual.

'Well, this is a mongrel. How much is the licence? I forget.'

Mr Hicks had found a licence form. Matilda could

hear him presently telling Mrs Hicks that Mrs Pollyput got a mongrel from the Lost Dogs when she could have had that Boxer almost free. They would sigh together over her folly.

'I shall call her Folly.' Mr Hicks was writing slowly, breathing hard through his well-picked nose, wide-nostrilled. 'Hairy as a fernfilled grotto.' Tom's voice from the past. None of her family liked Mr Hicks. Louise said he steamed open letters, Mark that he had bugged the call box outside – an unusual flight of fancy for Mark. 'How else could he know so much about every-thing?' She tried to hear Mark's voice but failed. Per-haps one only heard the voices of the dead? Anabel claimed that he had put his hand up her skirts at the school sports, a thick fingered hairy hand slowly filling in the form. Mr Hicks had all the time in the world.

'Folly, eh? And how is Claud?' Mr Hicks knew all about the postman's reign in Claud's affections and never hesitated to put in a reminding pin. Matilda, wait-ing for the man to finish writing the few words and find the date stamp, leafed through the paper.

'No sub-post offices robbed lately,' she said brightly.

'Busy murdering their mothers.' Mr Hicks brought the date stamp down hard on the dog licence. 'There's your Folly all legal.'

Matilda interpreted this as a quick dig against sex between consenting males. 'I don't feel matricide and robbery go together somehow. I haven't seen anything that he robbed his mother, only that he killed her.'

'Only!' Mr Hicks, still holding the dog licence between finger and thumb, stared at Matilda through his thick lenses which hid his piggy eyes, 'Only! That sort of man doesn't need to rob, he's rich, isn't he? A toff who went to Winchester and New College.'

'What a delightfully old-fashioned word – a toff.' Matilda regretted the days of long ago when sub-post offices were not guarded by barriers of glass. Mr Hicks, holding the licence in his horrible fingers, was safe. He held her in his power, fixed her with his glittering glasses. She could not snatch the licence and so she must wait for him to pass it through the hatch. Had those fingers pried up Anabel's parts? One could never tell when Anabel was lying, she was a compulsive liar whose highest flights of fancy often turned out to be true.

'Lots of our Trade Union leaders went to New College, Mr Hicks.'

'But not to Winchester.' Mr Hicks was studying the licence. 'That school should be closed. It breeds more commies than any other school in England. I read it in a book.' By 'book' Mr Hicks meant magazine. Matilda bit her lip.

'Your party too, Mr Hicks.'

'My party?' Mr Hicks, fingers holding the licence, rested behind the glass as he leaned on the counter to see her better.

'Fascist – anti-nig-nog.' Matilda could just reach and take the licence without seeming to snatch. 'Thank you so much, Mr Hicks. Lovely day.' She left the shop regretting her anger, for he would know, as he always knew everything, that she was angry and he would wonder why. Very likely he would set about finding out.

She took the licence from her purse and stuck it on a hook on the dresser. If the murderer had taken Folly with him it would be more money wasted. She perused the papers.

Nothing in the *Sun*. She turned to the *Express*. Ah, here was something. *Matricide's car found at Harwich. Search for him intensified in Scandinavia.* Fru Sonja Andersson from Copenhagen had identified the killer on the ship. Why had she not reported her suspicions to the Captain? She had not been sure at first, but now she was asked, as were some of her fellow-passengers, she was sure and so was the friend travelling with her.

Bully for you, Sonja Andersson. The *Mirror* had in its inner page *Matricide in Porn Capital*. Goody! Matilda, hearing a step, looked up.

'I thought you'd gone.'

'I thought you'd have a Panda car waiting.'

Folly greeted Matilda enthusiastically.

'I bought her a licence,' she said shamefacedly.

'She trusts us.'

'Mm, puts us to shame.'

'Anything in the papers?'

'Yes, your car's been found at Harwich and you were seen by passengers on the boat to Denmark. How's that?'

'My car? Where?'

'If you left the keys in it somebody's pinched it.'

'That's very helpful.'

'Look, *Matricide in Porn Capital*. That's helpful. Nothing in any paper except the *Express* and *Mirror*. Your story is stale; they've run it into the ground.'

'Maybe, but the police –'

'They never give up but other things take their time. Look, here's a story of a wife's disappearance. Naked. Just her footmarks in the sand leading inland, uphill away from her clothes and her honeymoon husband.'

'Aahh.'

'And this one. *Man ate dog for bet. Mr Hooper of Saxon Lane, Hertford, killed his wife's spaniel dog, skinned it, roasted it in butter and ate it with caper sauce. Says it tasted rather strong.*'

'The British public won't like that.'

'*Interviewed last night Mrs Hooper said, in tears, I shall divorce him.* Of course she must.'

'You're making it up.'

'I'm not.' Matilda handed Hugh the paper. 'Could you manage some bread and cheese and salad? I don't usually eat much lunch.'

'When I've recovered from the roast dog story.'

'No worse than Matricide. I'll pick a lettuce.' She paused in the doorway, her face in shadow. 'Incidentally, why did you do it?'

Hugh blushed. 'I'll tell you some time, not now.' He bent down, embarrassed, stroking Folly's ears.

'Please yourself.'

'And you can tell me why you really planned your picnic.'

'Easy – but not now either.'

Together they shied away from their fear and horror, their pain and remorse.

We have quite a lot in common, Matilda thought wryly as she chose a lettuce, pulled spring onions and radishes.

'How tall are you?'

'Why?'

'Clothes.'

'Oh, six foot one or two if I hold myself straight.'

'If you've finished eating you had better come up and change your clothes. I'll burn yours.'

'Why? I'm not so desperately dirty.'

'It isn't the dirt, it's the description. All England, all Europe for that matter, knows you are wearing blue socks, suede shoes, fawn corduroy trousers, a check shirt, red and white, a red scarf round your neck and that you wear your watch on your right wrist.'

'How exact.' Hugh took off his watch. 'There's a sun-burn mark.'

'We'll rub in shoe polish. Come on.'

Touching Tom's clothes Matilda felt detached. A year ago she could not have opened his cupboard or chest of drawers without gulps of hysteria. Now she picked out a white T-shirt, a blue pullover, pants, jeans, and handed them to Hugh. 'Try his shoes for size.' She pointed to a row of shoes. 'Give me your clothes.'

Hugh changed, dropping his clothes onto the floor while Matilda stood looking out of the window.

'How do I look?'

'Changed.' She eyed him carefully. 'Tom was very dark. He was thin like you.'

'I think I've lost weight on the run.'

'I daresay. Here's his watch. Put it on. It's a cheap Ingersoll, goes like a bomb and tells you the date.' She strapped it round his left wrist.

'What shall we do with mine?'

58

'I'll put it in the bowl in the hall. It's full of unwanted stuff, anything small and broken. We'll hide it under the world's nose.'

'How much nose does the world put in your door?'

'Very little. I can't help the occasional person. Nobody comes regularly. Tom and I put people off. They got the message and left us alone.'

'And when he died?'

'One needn't encourage people. Everyone comes to the funeral, then they leave you alone.'

'The children?'

'They have husbands or lovers. They came once or twice dutifully. I could see my grief bored them. Mothers are not supposed to be in love with your father – there's something indecent about it. They adore love and sex for themselves but for parents it's unnatural.'

'I see.'

'Do you?'

'Well, yes, I do. I'm not your child.'

'You could be if –'

'Only if you'd been a child bride.'

'You flatter me. Actually Tom and I never stopped squabbling in front of the children so they thought my grief hypocritical.'

'Quarrels are often an indication of love.'

'Tell that to Louise, Mark, Anabel and Claud.' Matilda picked up Hugh's discarded clothes. 'Found any shoes that fit?'

'These sneakers are fine but my feet are bigger than his.'

'Perhaps it will be safe to keep your own.' She was doubtful.

'They are a very common make.'

'All right, then.'

In the kitchen Matilda cut up the discarded clothes and fed the bits into the Rayburn. Hugh sat watching her profile as she worked. What have I let myself in for? he wondered. He tried to place her among the women of his world and failed.

In the afternoon sun the garden shimmered with heat.

'I shall have to water my vegetables. There's been no rain.'

'I'll help you.'

'You might be seen.'

'Couldn't I be a visitor?'

'It's not normal for me to have visitors.'

Matilda, putting the last sock into the Rayburn, sat back, her hands folded in her lap, silent.

People do shy away from the slightly loopy, Hugh thought. They don't know what to say. If they are harmless they leave them alone. Watching her lids droop, he wondered whether sitting upright she would snore.

They sat companionably, both tired by the emotions of the past days.

It was Folly who heard the footsteps, first pricking her ears and looking from Hugh to Matilda. Hugh listened. Someone coming—a child on bare feet? Footsteps coming rather slowly from the copse. Was it a trick? A spy? Whoever it was, was coming on steadily. Folly growled. Hugh half rose then sat down again. He was cut off from the passage door by Matilda and could be seen through the open door from the garden. The footsteps were on the flagstones now. Matilda's head jerked up. She cried out, rushed to the door. The footsteps stopped.

'Gus!' Matilda sprang out, swooping down in a birdlike movement. Her arms and Gus's flapping wings made patterns in the sunlight. Gus raised his proud head, honked loud, then laid it across Matilda's lap. She gathered him into her arms.

'Gus, oh Gus! How did you get here? Oh Gus, it's more than ten miles – your feet –' She stroked his neck, his back, his breast. She examined each foot. 'You hero!'

Hugh brought a bowl of water. The gander dipped his beak in the water, raised it high, looking at Hugh with an enraged blue eye.

'It's all right, Gus, he's a friend.' Gus snipped quickly at Hugh's wrist and dabbed his beak at Folly who backed into the house, tail between her legs. 'She's a

60

friend. Oh Gus, I betrayed you.' Matilda sat inelegantly, her legs apart, skirt riding up. Gus made throttling noises, weaving his sinuous neck against her throat, nibbling her ears, tweaking her hair.

'He's made a frightful mess on your skirt.'

'That's love.'

'Will it wash off?'

'It doesn't matter. It's marvellous to have you back. We need you.' She looked up at Hugh who was grinning. 'We need him to protect us from prying eyes. Mr Hicks, for instance.'

'Who is he?'

'The postmaster. He's an inquisitive menace, dangerous.'

Hugh noted that Matilda had said 'we'.

9

Watching Matilda with Gus, Hugh wondered whether they were as beautiful as Leda and the Swan. This up-to-date version touched him. Matilda, bare legged, in a crumpled dress, stroking the bird, her hand sliding down his neck from head to breast, her white hair flopping forward over his head while he nibbled at her ears. Now and again the bird stopped his attentions to peer at Hugh and hiss.

'There's some maize in the scullery. Could you find it?'

Hugh brought it, holding out a handful to the bird. Gus snipped his forefinger in a painful grip. Hugh kept his hand still. Gus held on while Hugh waited. After a while the bird released him and began to eat. Matilda watched the blood returning to Hugh's finger.

'He won't do that again.'

'I hope he won't, once is enough.'

'He will terrorize Folly.'

'I think she will be all right. She's not very brave, a rabbit scared her in your wood.'

'Let's see.'

In the room behind them Folly sat anxiously on the chair by the Rayburn.

'I think he will ignore her.'

'She will keep out of his way.'

'Doesn't he have a new owner?'

'Oh Lord!' Matilda sat up. 'He will come over to tell me Gus is lost.'

'He may telephone. Couldn't you telephone first?'

'Yes.' Matilda was examining Gus's feet. 'He doesn't seem footsore.'

'Could he have flown?'

'Not the world's greatest flyer. He can fly but doesn't.'

'The stream?'

'It goes nowhere near – oh yes, it does, it comes down from the reservoir and he was at the farm at the far end of it. That must be it. You clever, clever Gus.'

'So diddums swam and paddled the whole way home –'

'I know I'm soppy.' Matilda got up, eyeing the goose mess on her frock. 'Frightfully hard to get the stain out. Lucky this dress is old. I'll telephone.'

Hugh listened as she went indoors. He could hear her dialling. The dial whined six times. Not 999, not the police. The gander, having finished the maize, began preening. In the house Matilda was talking. After a few minutes the receiver was replaced with a bang. Hugh waited. The gander finished preening and tucked his head along his back, letting himself sink down on the path.

Hugh looked at the watch on his left wrist. Twenty-four hours ago he had got off a train and taken a bus to the port.

'What are you thinking about?' Matilda sat down beside him.

'What did the man say?'

'He said Gus was no good, attacked his geese, killed one. He *was* rude, said Gus is no gander, no good to him, and will I send a cheque for the damage! I said I would and to bugger off.'

'Wouldn't do for the W.I.'

'I told you.'

'Not a very successful betrayal.'

'No. What were you thinking just now?'

'How I was twenty-four hours ago.'

'Tell me.'

'I had been on the move since I killed my mother. I thought I might get to France, might meet someone with

63

a boat who would take me across. That's what I thought early on. Then I decided it was all too silly. I'd wait until dark and go out with the tide. The police have been no help at all.' Hugh laughed. 'I've discovered how to run away successfully in this country.'

'How?'

'For starters you don't mind whether you are caught or not. You never hurry. You ask the way, if possible from a policeman. He will obligingly tell you. I even went into a police station and stood by a wanted poster of myself and asked the way to the bus station. They gave me a lift in a Panda.'

'Where was that?'

'Salisbury, I think. If you run you are chased. If you wander about unworried nobody bothers.'

'You were just lucky.'

'No. The nearest I ever got to getting caught was when you started helping me.'

'Thanks!'

'I do. But now I don't want to be caught. I'm dead scared.'

'Oh.'

'I keep thinking you will send for the police. I thought when you went to the village that you would get them then, that I would find them waiting when I came back from the wood. I thought just now you might dial 999 not the goose man. I'm sorry.'

'Nothing to be sorry about. I'm a great betrayer.'

'Not really.'

'Half of me is. I hoped you'd be gone, taking Folly, when I came back from the village. I thought having a dog with you would be splendid camouflage. I didn't want to get involved and then –'

'Then?'

'Then I thought I do want to be involved, it's fun.'

'Fun? Who for?'

'Me. I've had no fun for years.'

'I wondered whether you were mad.'

'Menopause?'

'Yes.'

'No way – beastly expression – but it applies, it's true. This is fun, let's make a success of it.'

'Harbouring a murderer is a criminal offence. Don't be frivolous.'

'Don't be so conventional. People are conventional, we can't do without them. In your case, in my life, I've no room for it.'

'Oh.'

'If you want to go to the police yourself or throw yourself into the sea –' Matilda flushed, getting angry.

'And what will you do?'

'Kill Gus, have Folly destroyed, wait for the tide to be right and swim out as I'd planned.'

'Such despair.'

'We have equal despair. Your despair could cancel mine, that's all.'

'Blackmail now.'

'If that's what you like to call it.'

They stared at one another with horror.

'We are getting a bit near the knuckle,' Hugh murmured.

Matilda nodded.

Feeling their tension, the dog had got down from the safety of the chair and sat between them, managing to press her bony ribs against each of them. She shivered a little, eyeing Gus, but more fearful of losing Hugh and Matilda.

'It's all right.' Hugh stroked the dog's head. 'Nothing to worry about.'

'Sorry to be nervy.' Matilda was apologetic. 'It's Mr Hicks. There's something very unpleasant about that man. Maybe Anabel wasn't lying.'

'About what?'

'She said he groped up her skirts years ago. We couldn't believe her, but I don't know. He frightened the children. Today he made me uneasy. He pries through pebble glasses.' Matilda shivered. 'A goose walking over my grave. Not you, Gus, not you.' She looked at Gus,

65

folded compactly in sleep. 'Horrible Mr Hicks was one of the first on Louise and Anabel's list.'

'What list?'

'They took a great interest when they were about fifteen and eleven in the population explosion. It was about then Louise joined the Conservative Party. They hung a sheet of foolscap on the wall by the clock and listed people they would eliminate. Mr Hicks was high on the list. They ran out of actual people rather soon or changed their minds and reinstated them, but Mr Hicks and Charles Manson were constants. It became a little macabre. I objected.'

'Little girls?'

'Little girls, yes, but I found Tom often agreed with them. They switched from actual people to kinds of people. The list included spastics, lepers, brain-damaged people. Claud wrote in brain-washed, and Louise started it again – the very old, all the handicapped, all Communists. Then Anabel decided Berlinguer was rather dishy and stopped playing. Louise took the list up to her room and carried on alone. A world without weak or imperfect people is, she thinks, she still thinks, a better world. She's a Fascist, my child.'

'And your Tom's.'

'Yes, of course. Oh well.' Matilda shook herself. 'Louise is one of the reasons I was picnicking. It would be intolerable to be looked after by Louise, however right she may be about Mr Hicks.'

'Have you a terminal illness?' Mention of the picnic suggested this reason to Hugh.

'Haven't we all?' He could see by the set of her jaw he would get no other answer.

10

That evening there was a thunderstorm which solved the problem of watering the garden. Clouds gathered about six o'clock while Hugh and Matilda watched the news on television.

The pound was down – the Bank of England had intervened.

The meeting in Brussels –

The E.E.C. –

Unrest in Spain, Ethiopia, the Middle East, Africa – Cambodia –

China –

Students –

The earthquake in Central Asia –

The C.I.A. –

Our correspondent in Beirut reports that the Moslems and Christians –

Mr X, the honeymoon husband of Perranporth told the police that –

Mrs Y, the owner of the dog eaten by her husband was arrested by the police this morning and will be charged with grievous bodily harm –

Our correspondent in Cape Town reports Hugh Warner, the Matricide, was seen at the races by an intimate friend Mrs Vivian Briggs –

Here the television blanked out, lightning flashed, followed by a clap of thunder.

Matilda got up and tried a light switch. 'Power cut,' she said and tried the telephone. 'That's gone too. Who is this intimate friend, Mrs Vivian something?'

'I've no idea.'

The rain came down in noisy torrents. Outside the kitchen door Gus honked, defying the elements. Folly crept under the dresser.

Matilda ran round the house shutting windows against the rain whistling down venomously after holding off for so long. Thunder crashed overhead, then cracked and burst simultaneously with the lightning. She found candles to light the kitchen. Hugh drew the curtains. Gus stood in the doorway and Matilda let him into the scullery and closed the door to the garden. Hugh lit the candles.

Matilda stood with her back to the stove, her arms crossed, hugging herself, her dress stained with goose mess, her feet bare. In turn she warmed each foot against the stove, standing birdlike on one foot. Her hair was swept into a crest. She looked, he thought, like a print he had once bought of a Polish Fowl.

When the centre of the storm had moved a little way off Matilda asked again: 'Mrs Vivian something?'

Hugh shook his head. 'No idea.'

Some girl friend of yesteryear, thought Matilda. Some woman who would enjoy saying at parties, 'Oh, Hugh Warner – of course I know him well –' attracting attention to herself by dubious name dropping. It was the sort of thing Anabel did. She let her mind dwell briefly on her daughter and found her wanting. Anabel craved attention, always had, and so too did Louise who got more, being more beautiful than her sister. Two beautiful daughters, two good looking sons, thought Matilda. They shall find nothing of me to pick over, no surprises. Let them go on with their erroneous ideas. She smiled.

'What's the joke?'

'I was thinking of my children.'

'Funny?'

'I have left no secrets for them to pore over – burned my letters, destroyed all clues. I shall leave them nothing but a shed snakeskin.'

'You look like a Polish Fowl.'

'They are very rare nowadays.'

'Yes?' Hugh was delighted that she knew what a Polish Fowl was.

'A white topknot, sometimes known as the Tufted Hamburg.'

'Extinct,' said Hugh, laughing.

'Like me.' Matilda smiled. 'I am almost extinct.'

'Shall we have a bottle of wine? It would pass the time.'

'Okay.' Matilda took a candle to the larder. Hugh watched her bend down, reaching for a bottle, and thought that for her age she had good legs, a good bottom. He opened the bottle, poured the wine. Matilda sat opposite him in the candlelight. Overhead and all round the hills the thunder groaned and rumbled. The rain spat down.

'I am an habitual liar,' Matilda remarked conversationally. 'I find it almost impossible not to embroider. Anabel is as bad.'

Hugh nodded.

'When I said Tom went to Paris to meet a friend and you said he went to meet Death I thought that sounded so good I'd let it go. I lied by default. In fact I don't like Paris. Tom knew there was no question of my going with him. When he wanted to go to Paris he went on his own. The friends he was meeting were his friends, not mine. Neither Tom nor I thought he would meet death. That was not in our plans at all. He had a heart attack in the rue Jacob – dropped dead.'

Hugh stayed silent.

'The children were all grown up. They had their lives. We were busy still with ours but –' Matilda pushed her hair away from her face, drank some wine. A slight draught made the candles flicker. Her eyes looked dark in their sockets. 'But Tom and I were aware of what was coming. Tom called it "La dégringolade". He could not bring himself, as I do, to call it disintegration. You looked surprised when I talked of a wrinkled bottom. However well and fit you are the flesh grows old. We had been young together, loved, fought, had children, ups and downs, a tiring, insecure life but not a boring one. We talked to each other, Tom and I. We decided when we were still in our prime not to allow ourselves to crumble into old age where you are dependent on others, your powers fail, you repeat yourself, you become incontinent. The children try their best, then put you into an old people's home with nothing to look forward to but the geriatric ward. That is what we both minded about age, the keeping alive of useless old people. He and Louise used to have a game: how many children could eat if old people were allowed to die? Millions.'

Hugh watched her drink more wine. Presently she went on.

'We decided we would leave no mess behind, nothing for the children to quarrel over. We would leave no messages, we would not let them know us once we were dead. Our children were not interested in how we had lived or felt, so our letters – when we were in love we wrote many letters, people did – we would destroy them. If they are ever interested it will be too late, we said.'

'Rather nasty of you.'

'D'you think so? We didn't mean it, well, he didn't. Tom was not a petty person. I am. I would have liked the children to have been interested in us but they were only interested in Louise, Mark, Anabel and Claud.'

'Are they interesting people?'

'To themselves, certainly.'

Hugh was afraid he had interrupted the flow but Matilda went on.

'Sex had a lot to do with it. We thought when sex was no longer fun, no longer essential, we would push off.

The great thing for us was to go together, to time it right. Our death must come while we still slept well, ate without indigestion, still made love, while, in Muriel Spark's words we were still "in possession of our faculties".' She sipped her wine, holding the glass with both hands, her head raised, listening to the thunder. 'We were not prepared to put up with terminal illnesses. It seemed to us that the responsible thing was to end our lives at the right moment, go while the going's good.'

'Responsible?'

'Yes. Socially responsible in the same way as birth control.'

'Wasn't it selfish?'

'Certainly not. We planned to save other people trouble as well as ourselves. It was unselfish.'

'I see your point.'

'There were other things. We planned not to have another dog or cat when ours died.' Matilda cast an irritated eye toward Folly sitting facing the Rayburn, ears cocked, listening. She sighed and made a defeated gesture.

'Suddenly Tom died without me, before we were ready, while we still –'

'Still?'

'Still were enjoying life. We weren't ready. I should have swallowed my pills then, looked sharp about it. But I have betrayed him. I'm still here, damn it.'

'You were about to have a stab at it last night.'

'You deflate me, mock me. It wasn't just a stab, it was the real thing. I had tidied myself away. In my mind I was as good as dead.'

'Okay. What about Gus? What about that heroic bird coming back to find an empty house?'

'It never occurred to me that he would.'

'And it never occurred to you and Tom that he would drop dead in the rue Jacob, did it? A fine pair, I must say.' Hugh drank his wine, refilled Matilda's glass.

'You are detestable.'

71

'And I murdered my mother.'

'How much do you mind?'

'It's difficult to say.'

'Why?'

'She wasn't particularly happy. She never had been satisfied with anything. She was a frightened person –'

'I bet she was, with you about to bash her to death.'

'It wasn't me she was afraid of, it was –'

From the scullery Gus set up a loud honking. There was a rat-tat-tat at the door. Matilda gestured toward the inner door. Hugh went through to the hall where he stood, heart thumping. Folly barked shrilly.

'Who is it?' Matilda shouted.

'Only me, Mrs Pollyput, only me. Constable Luce.'

'She did betray me,' thought Hugh. 'The crafty bitch, keeping me talking, telling me that tripey tale.'

'Came to see if you are all right, been a power cut in the valley.'

'Here too.' Matilda sounded cool. 'Come in. Like some coffee?'

'Powerful honk that gander's got. He's a good watchdog.'

'Yes, he is.'

'Got a new dog I see.'

'Yes, I licensed her today. Coffee? Tea? Wine? I'll get another glass.'

'No, thank you. I must be on my way. Just wanted to see you were all right, you living all alone here. Must be lonely.'

'I love it.'

'So they tell me. My wife wouldn't do it. She thinks you're brave.'

'Or mad perhaps.'

'No, no, what an idea –'

'My children think I'm crazy.'

'Do they? Well, it's for you to suit yourself isn't it?'

'Yes.'

'Nice little dog. She's only a puppy.'

'She might be. I got a licence to be on the safe side.'

'Sensible that.'

'I've always been scared of you since you caught me with the car untaxed.'

'It was duty. I was sorry to do it so soon after Mr Pollyput's death.'

'That's what made me forget. Sure you won't have a drink?'

'No thank you, Mrs Pollyput. I must be going. I was going to call in on Mr Jones.'

'He'll be hiding under the bed.'

The constable laughed.

'Goodnight,' Matilda called, watching the policeman get back into his car. She shut the door. 'You can come back now, he's gone.'

They sat again at the table. Hugh refilled their glasses. 'I took mine out of the room with me.' He glanced at her sidelong.

'How clever. I didn't think of it. I offered him wine.'

'I heard you.'

'Where were we?'

'You were telling me about your well-planned death with Tom after your successful loving life together.'

'You sound acid.'

'Did you love him?'

'Of course I loved him. There was never anyone else. He was my first and only love.' As she spoke a puzzled expression flitted momentarily across her face.

'What is it?'

'Something I can't remember.'

'Another man?'

'I don't know. How odd. How strange. Why should I suddenly think –'

'What?'

'Some tussle, a sort of thrill. Good Lord, I can't remember. It must be something I've heard or read. It wasn't me, one of the girls perhaps or a friend. Something happened at a party in Bloomsbury. Not important.'

Hugh didn't believe her.

'Where did you meet Tom?'

'At a party in Kensington.'

'And you fell in love and lived happily ever after.'

'Yes.'

Hugh tipped his chair back and laughed.

'It's not possible to believe.'

'Why not?' Matilda snapped. 'Ask around, ask our friends.'

'No need,' said Hugh. 'It's a good story but it won't wash.'

Matilda looked blank.

'A person like you,' explained Hugh, 'with a happy past, nothing but lovely memories does not just walk into the sea.'

'I should have thought it rounded everything off nicely,' Matilda now was sour.

'Either,' said Hugh, watching her, 'you had a happy surface life, even deceiving yourself, or you didn't care except for your animals.'

'What!' Matilda almost spat at him.

'I've seen you with Gus. That's genuine feeling. You are trying not to let yourself love Folly here.'

'I shan't.'

'There you go. So passionate.'

'Well, animals –' Matilda left her sentence airborne.

'Animals are easier to love than human beings. Animals give you their whole heart, animals don't betray. Shall I go on?'

'No. I think I shall get us some supper.'

Hugh watched her moving about the kitchen, laying the table, preparing vegetables, rubbing garlic onto steak, grinding the pepper mill.

'I believe your Tom had somebody else in Paris.' Hugh watched the hands twisting the pepper pot.

'Oh no.'

'I suppose yes. Why don't we tell one another the truth? We met near Death, why don't we tell the truth as good Catholics do on their deathbeds?'

'It would be original.' She put down the pepper pot.

'So he had someone else in Paris.'

74

'Yes, he did.'

'You could have done something – gone with him, murdered the girl. I'm supposing she was younger than you.'

'Much younger.'

'He would have got over it. Did you know her?'

'Yes. Yes. I thought so.'

'So?'

'I did murder someone once.' Matilda looked at Hugh across the table. 'I never think of it. It was so quick.'

'So why not the girl in Paris?' Hugh wondered if this crazy woman who looked like a bird was lying.

'One could never kill one's own child.' Matilda's voice was low.

'Was it Anabel?' Hugh felt shock.

'Louise.' Matilda put the steaks under the grill.

'I thought she was happily married,' Hugh said stupidly.

'I never said happy. She was only happy fucking with her father. You like your steak rare?'

'Rare, please.' He breathed in hard.

'And do you like French mustard or more Truth with your steak?'

'I should like mustard and the story of the murder you did commit.'

'All right, as we are into Truth. It's not as interesting as incest.'

'But longer ago?'

'Much longer ago, almost forgotten.'

11

When the telephone rang Matilda lifted the receiver and
listened, her jaws working on a mouthful. Hugh listened
too.

'Hullo?'

'Matilda, your phone was out of order.'

'There's been a storm. What do you want, John?'

'Piers.'

'Look, I've never called you Piers in my life. What is
this?'

'My name is Piers. Call me Piers.'

'Okay. What do you want?'

'I've got to go away. I want to know if you are coming
to London.'

'I might.' She swallowed the steak and held the
receiver away from her ear. Hugh listened to the
pedantic voice at the other end.

'Do make up your mind.'

'I can stay somewhere else.'

'You always stay here. I'd like to see you.'

'That's nice of you, John.'

'Don't tease. When are you coming?'

'I'll think. I'll let you know. I have to arrange for the
animals.'

'I thought the dog and cat were dead.'

'They are. Their names were Stub and Prissy, John.
They had names.'

'Well then? Come on, Matty, don't dither.'

'I'm not even going to try to call you Piers if you call me
Matty.'

'Sorry, Matilda.'

'I'll let you know. I'll phone.' She grinned. 'You wouldn't exactly call this an adult conversation, would you? Think what it's costing you, Piers. Goodnight.' She put down the receiver. 'I can fetch your money if you like. How would that be?' she asked Hugh.

'Marvellous.'

'Will you tell me where it is?'

'Yes.'

'My steak's cold. Damn! I'll give it to Fol-de-rol.' She cut the meat into small pieces.

'You were going to tell me about your murder.'

'So I was. It will give you a hold over me perhaps. John "Piers" knows about it.' She fed the bits of steak to Folly who took each piece delicately.

'Did your husband know?'

'No, come to think of it, he didn't. It never arose. Only John knows.'

'What happened?'

'It was that terrible winter after the war. You'd be too young to remember.'

'I don't. My mother talked of it.'

'I was nineteen, just married. First love. Marvellous. So great it hurt, every nerve raw with love. We had rushed into love, into marriage, headlong. It was gorgeous. I was pregnant with Louise. We were the only people in the world. Then I found he'd had this woman. She was older than him. She was all the things I wasn't. Well dressed, well read, travelled, sophisticated, good looking, sexy, funny, educated. She never let go of anyone she had once had. Once hers he was hers for evermore. She tormented me, showed me up naïve, unsure, inexperienced, unsafe. Tom used to laugh, said she didn't matter, never had, but I could see there was still a bit left over. If she jerked the lead he'd go back. I saw her do it to other men. Their girls could do nothing.' Matilda made a cross with her knife on a smear of butter. She seemed far away.

'What happened?'

77

'What? Oh! Yes, what happened. London was thick with snow. I was trying to get home to Chelsea from Marble Arch. All the buses were full. I couldn't get a taxi. It was dark, freezing hard, snowing, the ducks standing about on the ice. The snow blotted everything out. I walked through the park. Then, as I walked along the Serpentine towards Knightsbridge barracks, there she was. We were nose to nose in the snow. She laughed when she saw me. Her face lit up with pleasure. "My Tom's little wifey," she said. "Does he let you out alone?"'

Matilda laid her knife and fork side by side and looked across at Hugh. 'It annoyed me.'

'So?' He studied her face while she paused.

'So I hit her.' Matilda was now back there, standing in the snow by the Serpentine. 'I hit her as hard as I could. She was taller than me. She slipped down the edge onto the ice, tried to get her balance, slid on out, then, crack, she went through, disappeared.'

'What did you do?'

'I waited for her to pop up but she didn't. I suppose she went sideways under the ice. I ran all the way to John's house. He lived off Sloane Street in those days. He was in when I banged on the door. I told him what I'd done. He'd just got in, he was shaking the snow off his bowler and swishing his umbrella. I remember that clearly. He's a fussy old bachelor, wants me to call him Piers now. It suits him, his new job. He's hoping to get a knighthood. Sir Piers would be grander than Sir John. I tease him.'

'What did he do?' Hugh suppressed a longing to kick her shins.

'Oh. He made me sit down, gave me a stiff brandy, listened to what happened, then said I was not to tell Tom, ever. He asked me if anyone had seen it happen. I didn't think so. It was snowing so hard I couldn't see more than a few yards, in fact I'd hardly seen her fall through the ice, I only really heard it. Well,' she stood up, 'that's all. John took me home to Tom in his car, said

78

he'd overtaken me in the street. Tom was pleased to see me. I cooked dinner. It was steak, I remember that, black market. It was delicious.'

Hugh allowed the pause to lengthen.

'I suppose the snow covered your footprints.'

'I suppose it did.'

'When was she found?'

'When it thawed, weeks later. Tom read it in the paper at breakfast. He said, "Oh look, old Duplex is dead. Found drowned in the Serpentine." Old Duplex was her pet name, her real name was Felicity.'

'What did you say?'

'I can't remember. I remember it being quite obvious he didn't care one way or the other so I had no remorse.'

'And Sir Piers?'

'He's like the grave. He's never referred to it. Funny fellow.'

'Was he in love with you?'

'John? He's not capable of love. He's cold.'

'The police?'

'John clammed up and I forgot all about it. I've never told anyone until now.'

'It's a good story.'

'Yes,' said Matilda kindly, 'a good story. You see, anybody can commit murder. It's chance really.' She could see Hugh didn't believe her or was uncertain.

'You are uncertain of my veracity.'

'A bit. It seems odd you should meet this Felicity woman alone in Hyde Park in the snow.'

'Not really. She used to follow me to make me feel uncomfortable. One never knew when or where she would appear. She did it to other women whose husbands had lain with her. It was her hobby to make us feel insecure. John told me. I remember now when he gave me the brandy he said, "A lot of girls will be the happier. You must not let it worry you. Promise." I'd forgotten that. I promised – put it right out of my mind.'

'Can you do that? Put things aside.'

'One has to.' Matilda looked bleak. 'I put Louise aside.

How else could I have gone on living with Tom? He needed me, I needed him and Louise –' Her voice trailed, leaving Louise up in the air. She got up and began clearing the table.

'Let's have some coffee and you tell me where your money is hidden. I'll stay a night or two with John and fetch it for you. Is it somewhere difficult to get at?'

'No, it's under the carpet on the staircase up to my flat.'

'For everyone to tread on?'

'Yes.' Hugh smiled.

Matilda's laugh rang out in delight.

'How original.'

'It was my brother's idea, some of it is his. Tax evasion.'

'So he –'

'No, he won't. My mother had just heard he was missing in Guerrilla country.'

'Dead?'

'For his sake one hopes so.'

'Oh, Guerillas/Gorillas. Your poor mother. Maybe I'm right, she was lucky. Did she love him?'

'He was her whole life.'

'There you are then, you did the right thing.'

'She could have loved me more.'

'Too big a risk, I think.' He could see Matilda's thoughts straying where he could not follow. 'No more risks for me.' Her face was dead-pan. 'Bed for me. We can plan your future tomorrow. I will ring up the soon-to-be Sir Piers and tell him I'm coming.'

'But –'

'We've had enough for one day.' Hugh watched her trail up the stairs. Folly stayed with him until he too climbed up the stairs and, while he took off his clothes, she turned several times around, pulling the duvet into a lump with her paws, waiting for him to get into bed. He held her close to his chest, stroking the silky ears while he tried not to think of Matilda's pain. The dog sighed, breathing warm air into his neck while he lay sleepless,

80

listening to the summer night. He wondered whether
Matilda considered God, as his mother professed to do,
or whether Death was her only certainty where there
would no longer be the possibility of love dying? And did
she love Louise, Mark, Anabel and Claud? She had loved
her husband. Her voice altered when she spoke the
name Claud. He would study it if he had time perhaps.
Blood relationships inclined to surprise when there was
the inability to communicate.

12

When Hugh woke the sun was up. Below his window he could hear the gander talk, Matilda answer. The bird stood on the brick path watching Matilda hoeing along a line of spinach, her movements brisk, economical.

Hugh pulled on his trousers and shirt and opened the door into the passage. Matilda's door was open, the bed unmade. Hugh looked again at the cupboard, parting the dresses on the rail to see how large a space lay behind. Satisfied, he prowled round the room, glancing at her things; a silver mirror, a brush, few pots or bottles on the dressing-table. He opened a drawer full of bras and nylons. Remembering his mother's habits, he tried the bedside table, found what he sought, a pile of snapshots. Tom, tall, handsome, fine eyes, hawkish nose, something fanatical about the mouth, a mouth that had kissed wife and daughter. Other snaps jumbled up of children, dogs, Matilda with the children, Matilda holding a puppy, scrawled on the back 'Stub – three months'. She held the animal with more care than she did the children. Another snapshot – Tom with Louise. The photograph had been crumpled, then smoothed out. Hearing Matilda come into the house he shut the drawer, went down to the kitchen.

'Sleep well?' She looked fresh, healthy.

'Very well thanks. I was prowling round upstairs. I saw you in the garden.'

'It's the best time to do chores. I'll get breakfast.'

'Have you any photos of your family?'

Matilda looked up. 'Try the dresser drawer. There's

an envelope on the left, taken before they all flew.'

'Flew?'

'Birds leave the nest. It's the best thing.'

Hugh opened the drawer, found an envelope. 'Is this it?'

'Yes. I don't much care for snaps. It's other things which bring them to mind – smells, sounds, materials.'

'Claud's dresses?'

She laughed. 'Of course, his dresses. That's me. Younger.'

A younger Matilda stared at the camera, her hair blown across one eye. 'That's Louise with Pa.' The voice was dry. Louise, tall, exquisite, standing close, too close to her father. 'Anabel.'

'Oh, Anabel. It's a bit blurry.'

'It's very good of Stub and Prissy.'

Anabel lay by the dog and cat who stared from eternity with enigmatic eyes. Another of Anabel, a better one – one wouldn't get much change out of her. He put the snap down and picked up the last. Two exquisite girls in jeans, long fair hair, laughing eyes, long narrow legs, the one on the left so beautiful she leapt from the snapshot, so desirable she moved him.

'That's Claud – he's still like that.'

'I'm bowled over.'

'Everyone is.'

'No wonder he made trouble for the girls.'

'There's always trouble,' Matilda said.

'You love him the best.'

'I do.' Matilda picked up the snapshots and put them away. 'Yes I do.'

Outside the house Gus honked. Matilda motioned Hugh out of the room.

'You in, Mrs Pollyput?'

'Yes.'

Hugh slid into the hallway.

'Post.'

'Oh, George, thank you. Only bills I bet.'

Hugh saw a man's shadow, heard steps.

'Looks like Claud's writing.'

83

'George, you are unethical. Like a cup of tea? Postmen shouldn't pry.'

'Wouldn't say no.' A chair scraped on the stone floor. Hugh risked a quick glance and stifled a laugh. This Claud's postman? Large head, massive shoulders, ginger hair getting thin, a heavy brutish face.

'How is Rosie?'

'In whelp again.'

'George, don't be crude.'

'She's a bloody bitch, Mrs Pollyput.'

'George, shut up! You love her. You are very happy.'

'If you say so.' George sounded sulky.

'I do say so. It's no use pretending anything else.'

'It's just this, Mrs Pollyput. Things might have been different. I feel trapped married, like every other fellow. Now it'll be three kids. I might – well, when I see his writing, I just think, that's all.

'When you see Claud's writing you should thank your lucky stars that Claud left you. God knows what would have happened. Get on with your job, George. You had a sniff of sulphur – be thankful for Rosie.'

'You are right. I daresay it was the glamour.'

'He's not really glamorous, he's a clown. He says here on this postcard he is hard up. Did you read it? I bet you did. Hard up means he's been chucked out of another job or has quarrelled with his feller.'

'Oh, Mrs Pollyput.'

'Still owes you, does he? How much?'

'Never mind, Mrs Pollyput. I'm sorry I read the card. It set me remembering.'

'Push off, George. Give my love to Rosie.' Footsteps faded, Gus honked, Matilda sighed.

'Claud's postman?' She glanced at Hugh. 'Rather unlovely.'

'He picks them for contrast. Dreadful boy.'

'Don't pay his debts.'

'Goodness no!' Matilda sighed again. 'Now. Let us be clever, make lists and timetables so that you know when to make yourself scarce, where to hide and when you

84

are safe. You must keep out of sight until you have your money and the hunt has died down. Then if you want to move on you can.'

'If you really mean it. Tell me your daily routine. I can memorize. For the unexpected I can improvise but I am worried about any consequences for you.'

'I've told you,' Matilda snapped, 'I'm enjoying it. Don't you see, you've given me something to do. A bit of life, for Christ's sake. I was bored stiff.'

'Okay, okay, let's make a list then. What happens from morning till night.'

Matilda made a list, starting with the postman at the same time each day as she was finishing breakfast so that he could be fairly sure of an offer of tea. 'I owe it to him. Claud behaved very badly.'

'Was it first love?'

'It was for George. Claud's first love is Claud. He can only hurt himself.'

'And your first love was Tom?'

'Yes.'

'Are you sure?'

'Of course I am.' Matilda was overemphatic.

'There must have been others before him. When you were a child were you not in love?'

'No.' Again the emphasis. Hugh waited.

'There is a rota of postmen. When it's not George's turn they come before I am up. I never see them so you won't have to bother about them.'

'Okay.'

'The milk comes Mondays, Wednesdays and Fridays. You hear the van, Gus honks, you can keep out of sight. The dustbin men come round Thursdays. You hear them miles away. That's about all. I do my shopping in the village or the town.'

'Where we met.'

'Yes.'

'Anyone else?'

'Mr Jones. He gives a shout when he's some way off. He's nervous of Gus. If I don't answer he goes away.'

'Sure?'

'Yes. Quite often I don't answer. He can be a bit of a bore.'

'Made a pass at you?'

Matilda blushed. 'I'm too old.' She caught Hugh's eye. 'Well, he did, but I took evasive action. One must be kind. He's got the male menopause, Claud says. Louise said the same thing.'

'What other neighbours?'

'Few. They wave as they go by, shout "How are you?" or "It's a fine day." Gus keeps them away. Nobody cares to get nipped. Gus will warn you.'

'What about exercise for me?'

'I hadn't thought.'

'I'll walk at night.'

'That would never do. Everyone would know. Dogs would bark. You'd be seen.'

'I can't stay cooped up. I'll go mad.'

'You'd be cooped up in prison.'

Hugh did not rise to this bait. 'I'll play it by ear,' he said.

'All right.' Matilda agreed, then, remembering another danger, said: 'Never ever answer the telephone. That would be fatal.'

'Do many people ring up?'

'No, but if I go to London and collect your money and you answered the telephone it would be known there was someone in the house.'

Hugh was bored by this meticulous planning.

'Suppose you carry on exactly as though I were not here – let me keep out of sight. If someone does come in say I'm a friend of Claud's or something.'

'You are not his type. I'd say Mark, a friend of Mark's.'

'He has catholic tastes?' Hugh was pleased not to be suitable fry for Claud.

'Mark is straight hetero.' Matilda smiled. 'No problem there.'

'I thought this Mr Jones fed Gus for you when you go away –'

'He thinks I've given him away.'

'Won't he find out?'

'Damn! Of course he will. When I go you'll have to avoid him.'

'I expect I shall manage. What would you be doing if I were not here?'

Matilda glanced at the kitchen clock. 'I'd go to the village, do a little shopping, come home, have a snack, work in the garden, snooze in the sun, go to the sea if it's fine.'

'Then why don't you do just that?'

'There's you.'

'Don't bother about me. Let me manage. I'm not half-witted. If you go to London I will be deeply grateful. I swear I won't be seen. Why not go and do your shopping – carry on as usual?'

Matilda looked doubtful, then agreed. Hugh watched her drive down the lane with relief, glad to have the house to himself. The fuss she was making was tedious, all the more irritating since he felt he should be grateful.

He sighed and set about exploring the house. He felt it impossible to believe Matilda had really swept herself away. There must be clues to her character that she was unconscious of leaving. He remembered exploring his home as a child, his discoveries among his parents' possessions. The thought of his mother, lovely, young, made him pause. She had been old looking up from the sofa, really old. The recollection of her sitting there, eyes full of terror rid him of any wish to pry on Matilda. He would do it later, in a better mood. He wandered back to the stream in the copse, Folly at his heels. If he stared long enough at the running water he would stop seeing his mother's hands, rings loose on old fingers. The rings, in his childhood, had fitted tight. She had pulled hard to get them off. 'Try them on your thumb, my love,' she had said. 'Try them on your thumb.' He looked at his hands. None of those rings would fit now. He sat watching the water flow past, the dog beside him, companionable, alert, quizzing a black and green dragonfly zipping up and down the water.

Presently Gus floated past, proudly paddling.

'Goose murderer,' Hugh called to the bird. 'Goose assassin.' Gus barely turned his head, floating on to land further down to crop grass on the bank.

'Thinks he's human,' Hugh said to the dog. 'Thinks himself like us, free to take life.' The dog looked up at him briefly, then lay in a ball against his thigh, her nose under her tail, the warmth of her body consolatory.

Gus finished cropping grass, crossed the stream and waddled back to the cottage past Hugh who heard him honk as a car passed along the lane.

The gander set up a different honking when Matilda returned. Hugh heard her voice raised in greeting. Followed by the dog, he went to meet her.

'I've bought stocks of food for you for when you're alone. Tins and dry stuff. You won't have to shop. I won't be away long. D'you think you can manage with cold food?'

'Oh yes.'

'If you have the fire the village will see smoke and if I'm away someone may come and look.'

'I'll be all right.'

'It's rather drear but –'

'Less drear than the nick.'

'There's that. Oh, by the way, Mr Jones – he sees UFOs.'

'What?'

'UFOs. He's given up telling the police because they laugh but he still tells me. It's just possible that he may appear suddenly then –'

'What do you do about it?'

'I pretend to take an interest. Tom did. He always took note; it's a neighbourly act.'

'Do I hide?'

'He can appear silently on bare feet. It's awkward. Even Gus has missed him on occasion.'

'It's a hazard I must take.'

'Yes.'

Gus honked. 'Telephone.' Matilda ran to answer it.

'Hullo? Oh darling!' – a cry of joyful greeting. 'How lovely to hear your voice. Where are you? In England . . . how long for? Oh . . . shall I see you? Oh, I see . . . yes, of course, too busy . . . no, no, of course you must . . . yes . . . no . . . no, of course not . . . yes, I'm well, of course I am . . . yes . . . no . . . really? . . . well, best of luck, it sounds a brilliant idea,' quite honest too . . . what? . . . I said quite honest too . . . must rush . . . goodbye.' He heard the telephone ping as she rang off. Several minutes passed before she came outside.

'That was Claud.'

'Too busy to see you?'

'Yes. He has a new venture. So like Claud. It's brilliant. I hope it makes him lots of lolly.'

'I talked to my mother like that.' Hugh watched her.

'Me too, but I hated mine and she me, whereas Claud –'

'Is too busy.'

'I had to be quick to be the first to ring off.'

'I noticed.'

'I used to drag on until he said, "I must go now, Mama." I've learned. I've learned to be the first to ring off.' She looked sidelong at Hugh for approval. 'It's hard learning not to be a bore. I damn near invited him to my funeral but –' She began to laugh.

'What's the joke?'

'His new venture. He's buying up old gravestones with beautiful inscriptions to sell to Americans. He's going up to Yorkshire where they are turning several graveyards into car parks.'

'Who sells them?'

'Oh, I wouldn't ask!' Matilda broke into cheerful giggles. 'An impoverished curate perhaps? The Church of England doesn't pay well, so –'

'If you found some round here?'

'I'd see him then of course. He might even stay the night and charge up the County Hotel to an expense account.'

Hugh said nothing.

'It does prove it's time to be off.' Matilda sounded almost pleased as she reversed disappointment to hope.

'To London?'

'To the next world.'

'Will he phone again?' Hugh found himself hating Claud.

'No, no, that's my ration.'

13

Two days passed. The weather stayed hot. Her feeling
of trepidation subsided; Matilda grew calm. Hugh gave
no trouble. He ate sparingly, slept a lot, spent hours out
of sight in the copse with the dog. In a conscious effort to
act normally Matilda worked in the garden, shopped in
the village, read the papers, watched television, went to
bed, got up at her usual time, cleaned the house in a
desultory manner and cooked meals for herself and
Hugh. She decided on action.

'I must ring up John/Piers, he always gives me a bed
in London. Tom and I always stayed with him. He was
my friend but became more Tom's. I'll telephone tonight
and fix it. It's a very comfortable house. Perhaps you
know him? John seems to know everybody, he's very
social.'

'No, never heard of him.'

On the line from London John was warmly welcoming.
Of course she must come. When? Soon? 'Come soon, I'm
going away, come before I go. I'm very busy but we can
have the evenings together.'

'That would be nice.'

'How long can you stay?'

'Oh, not long, a night or two.'

'Nonsense, you must stay at least ten days, get back
into your London ways. Mrs Green will give you breakfast in bed. We will cosset you.'

'Would Monday be all right?'

'Of course. I shall expect you in time for dinner. You'll
take the usual train?'

'I expect so.'

'Monday evening then.' John rang off.

Matilda looked at Hugh. 'Did you hear him? He has a very loud voice, always has had.'

'Every word. What does he do?'

'Some branch of the Treasury. He wanted the Foreign Service. He was disappointed. We met when we were young. His aunt was a friend of my mother's. He's rich, rather an old woman, likes his comforts, won't ever come here, it's not grand enough. He likes birds and fishing. Tom and I could never decide whether he liked girls or boys or neither. That side of him is non-existent, he's sexless.'

'Or it's carefully hidden.'

'That's what Tom said – carefully hidden. He always pretends he is something to do with Intelligence, it's his sort of snobbery.'

'What form does it take?'

'He talks as though he knew about spies, defectors to and from Russia, the C.I.A., French Intelligence, even Chinese. To hear him talk he might be all the M.I.s rolled up in one umbrella. He carries an umbrella, wears a bowler.' Matilda laughed. Hugh liked to see her laugh; she had small teeth, unhorsey.

'He's an odd man,' Matilda went on, 'good-looking in a way. He always talks as though he knows me better than I know myself. He also knows the children better. He knew Tom better, too.'

'Differently, perhaps?'

'Perhaps that's it. Another side to the side which was mine? People are so much more difficult than animals.'

'You love animals best?'

'Oh yes,' she said quickly. 'I trust animals.'

'Not Tom? You didn't trust Tom?'

Matilda flushed.

'I'm sorry,' Hugh said quickly. 'I'd forgotten.'

'I didn't trust Tom before I found him in bed with Louise. There was a part of Tom I never knew and John, in an odd way, knew it. He knows more about Mark,

92

Claud, Anabel and Louise than I ever shall.'

'Why does John want to be called Piers? Does he hate his name?'

'No.' She shook her head. 'He wants to be Sir Piers, it's more elegant.'

'Are you afraid of him?'

'He is a bit creepy. Claud says he's creepy. When the children were small he pretended he knew all about Burgess, Maclean and Philby. The children called him "Beclean filthy". A silly joke.'

'How well does he know you?' Hugh wondered whether Matilda would tell this man about himself.

'We've known each other since we were tots. I don't tell him things, not since I killed Felicity. I've been very careful since that episode.'

'Maybe there's some other thing?'

'What could there be?' Hugh watched her puzzled face and a minute breeze of fear flickered in her eyes. She also seemed puzzled. I'm getting to know this woman, he thought then. 'Let me tell you where the money is.'

'Yes, do.'

'If I give you my latchkey could you get me a pair of my own shoes?'

'Of course.'

'What else shall you do?'

'Get my hair done, shop.'

'Don't let them spoil it!'

'If I go looking like this John won't take me to good restaurants. He'll say nothing and take me to cheap, pokey places, hide me.'

'Nasty man.'

'Just vain. He likes to be seen with presentable women.'

'Not Polish Fowls.'

'Certainly not.'

'He doesn't like animals best.'

'I don't think he likes animals at all, or people. He is the sort of person who likes power. Poor old boy, it would be nice for him to be Sir Piers. That would give him a certain power. Sir Piers first, then after a few years Sir Piers will shift into another gear. Who knows – KCMG? I think he would like that.'

She is being malicious, Hugh thought and wondered whether Matilda knew she did not like this man or whether she had buried her feelings too deep to germinate.

'Shall you see friends?'

'I have so few left in London.'

'That's no answer.'

'We, or I, have changed. There isn't much left in common.'

'Your other children?'

'Neither Anabel nor Mark are in London.' She straightened her back. 'I wouldn't know if they were.'

'Surely?'

Matilda grinned. 'Did you keep your mother posted?'

'No,' he said. 'I did not bother.'

'She had her cat.' Matilda's unkindness was intentional.

'You need not invite me to your funeral either,' he said.

'Love all.' She pursed her lips.

14

When Matilda set off, respectable in her London clothes, Hugh sighed with relief. He intended a voyage of exploration. He was still sure that he would find some clues about to amuse him during her absence.

In the dressing-table drawers were the photographs – Louise, Mark, Anabel and Claud from babyhood to adolescence. He turned them over. Sometimes something was written on the back – 'Mark in Berlin' or 'Picnic near Helston'. In a good-looking family Claud's beauty was outstanding. He was like Matilda, but beautiful. He put the photographs aside, feeling that he knew Claud, would not care for Louise, would like to fuck Anabel, be bored by Tom and really dislike Mark who had a priggish expression. He searched for letters but was not rewarded. He put the snapshots back. There was a space in the drawer where probably Tom's letters had lain – now destroyed? No sign of any in Matilda's writing. At the back of the drawer a yellowed postcard of Trafalgar Square. 'Come at the same time. I'll take you on to the party. It's in Guildford Street.' No signature, but Hugh was reminded of the voice on the telephone which he had heard, 'You will take the usual train.' The postcard was in an authoritative script. He put it back.

Hugh prowled, felt the bed, a deep mattress. He examined her books. There had been a poetry phase. Then, rather surprisingly, the Russians: Chekov, Dostoevsky, Tolstoy. Then Camus and Sartre. The flyleaf of each book was initialled and dated. She had tried Bertrand

Russell but not got far, had read Thomas Mann, left Jane Austen untouched but managed Shaw. Graham Greene and Muriel Spark were read and reread. In Ivy Compton-Burnett she had written on a flyleaf, 'needs more concentration than Dostoevsky.' In Margaret Drabble's first novel, in Claud's hand, 'Darling Mama, try this, she knows about your kind of despair.'

Hugh opened Matilda's drawers. The clothes were not the clothes of a woman who felt the need of sexy knickers. She wore Indian cotton shirts as nightdresses, Jaeger wool tights in winter. The clothes were rather worn, unglamorous. In the middle dressing-table drawer a note: 'Have put jewels in the bank, listed for each of you. Don't quarrel – take what's given. I flogged the pearls.' That wouldn't make much difference with Matilda dead, Hugh felt. There was an envelope with a bent corner as though it had been stuck in the corner of the mirror. Hugh tried it. The crease fitted. He went downstairs and put the kettle on to steam the envelope open. Inside on a plain sheet of paper dated the day he had met her was a note:

Darling Louise, Mark, Anabel and Claud. I have had enough. Please have me cremated and scatter my ashes over the stream. I love you all. I am in full possession of my faculties. My Will is at the bank. Goodbye. I love you. Don't feel guilty. Your loving Mother.

Hugh wondered why she had said twice that she loved them. It tinged of doubt. He stuck down the envelope and went back to the room to replace it. He closed the drawer and lay down on Matilda's bed. Folly, who had kept silent company, got up and lay sighing, pressing her nose against his neck, her breath warm and damp.

'She must be about fifty.' Hugh put his arm round the dog. 'She hasn't quite swept herself out of the house,' he whispered to the dog. 'She left her anxieties about their subsequent behaviour. Poor fare.' Hugh sighed and repeated 'poor fare' which made him feel hungry. Matilda would be arriving in London about now. 'Let's get some food and then get out.' He stroked the dog who was making a draught with her tail.

Downstairs he fed her, made tea and ate a tin of tuna fish with pepper and raw onion, then lay again on Matilda's bed until it grew dark.

He let himself out of the back door, locked it and set off across the fields, desperately in need of exercise.

He walked up the valley, taking his bearings by the stars. The air was clear, the country very still. Walking across the fields, trying not to disturb sheep and cattle, he zigzagged to find gates, kept on uphill. Cars drove occasionally along the lane but he kept below the sky-line, gaining confidence as he walked, feeling his unused muscles working easily. Near the top of the valley he came to the village – a post office, one pub, a church, scattered houses, two farms in the village itself. He debated whether to try and skirt round but decided to walk through. It was September, there would still be holiday people about, he would not be conspicuous. The pub was surrounded by parked cars, a cheerful hubbub came out of open windows. Dogs barked as he passed the farmyards. Folly closed in on his heels. From the houses came the sound of television, music and loud laughter. Beyond the village a stretch of road, then a wood, a stile, a path sign-posted. He climbed the stile and followed the path, disturbing a pair of lovers. It led through the wood, over a stretch of moor to the top of a hill, turning left downhill. He stopped to get his bearings. Below and behind him lights from scattered houses and farms, the headlights of cars probing along the main road, far off the red glow of the town. To his right, away from the path and below it was a long reservoir, silver from the rising moon slicing the black water. He jogged down-hill to the water's edge. Folly drank. Hugh felt the temperature of the water. He listened. There was no sound other than faint rustling in the reeds.

His mother, he remembered, as he crouched with his hand in the water, had told him that in her youth, sent to Germany to learn the language, she had swum at night in the lakes. He remembered her voice.

97

'We swam naked, darling. If we rode we took off the saddles and swam the horses. We held on to their manes and they drew us along. It was poetry.'

Hugh had been delightedly shocked, unable to imagine his mother so.

'Naked?'

'Yes, darling, naked boys and girls. Of course our parents thought we were all in bed.'

'Together?' Hugh had asked. His mother had said:

'Don't be improper. Of course not.'

'Wasn't the swimming improper then?'

'It didn't feel it. They were all young Nazis, strength through joy and so on, handsome creatures. Their father was a Graf – very pro-Hitler for a while.'

'But Grandfather!'

'Your grandfather sent me there to get a good accent. When I wrote to him about the Strength through Joy he came at once and fetched me home. He'd never bothered about the quarter of Jewish blood in my mother before, never thought about it.'

'Poor mother.'

'Well, the swimming was lovely, you should try it some time in a lake at night.'

He took off his clothes and waded into the water, trying not to make a splash. Folly followed. They swam out together. The dog came too close and scratched his shoulders. Hugh swam out to the middle of the reservoir, thinking of his mother, trying to visualize her swimming in Germany, but it was Matilda he thought of who, having had enough, had been about to swim out to sea. He turned back to find his clothes. He dressed while Folly shook herself and rolled in the rough grass by the water's edge.

He walked back slowly, astonished at the distance he had covered on his walk. His mother was right, the swimming was good. He decided to do it again. There was no need to tell Matilda, who would worry and push her hair up in a crest. What had she had enough of, he wondered? Loneliness? People adjusted to being alone.

98

Was she bored? Certainly not ill. She appeared to have the wherewithal to live without undue worry. Guilt? Not guilt – she barely remembered killing that woman – he was half inclined not to believe it. What then? What? He was very tired when he got near the cottage, anxious for food and sleep. In his scullery Gus honked loudly. Hugh stopped. Gus could not have heard him yet. Folly pricked her ears. Hugh stood at the edge of the copse. A figure was creeping round the cottage, a short thickset man with a beard. He peeped in at the windows, funnelling his eyes with both hands to look in, moving from window to window, trying the back door. Gus honked.

'All right, all right, I hear you. She out or something? Not like her to be going out.' The voice was faintly Welsh. 'She can't be away or she would have asked me to look after you.' He was now peering in at the scullery window, standing on an upturned bucket to look in. Gus flapped his wings.

'All right then, all right. I'll be round again tomorrow, eh?' The visitor stepped off the bucket and set it right way up. Hugh watched him walk away, waited for him to be well out of sight before letting himself into the house. Gus throttled in his throat in greeting.

'Mr Jones, was it? Seen a UFO or something? I'd forgotten about him.'

Not daring to put on a light in case the man came back, Hugh felt his way about the kitchen, finding the bread, butter, a bottle of beer in the larder, cheese.

He sat at the table munching, still thinking of Matilda. Despair? Self-hate? Maybe. Hugh shrugged his shoulders, climbed the stairs. He went into Matilda's room, got into her bed with Folly. She had not changed the sheets, they were rumpled, the pillow smelled of her hair. He felt comforted. It was on this pillow she snored open-mouthed.

15

The ringing telephone woke Hugh. He had overslept; it was late, nearly ten.

He let the thing ring. He had promised Matilda not to answer it. They had arranged a code. If it rang three times and stopped it would be Matilda. She would do this twice. The third time he would answer, otherwise he would let it ring unanswered.

When the phone stopped Hugh went down to let Folly out and feed Gus his mush by the back door, which he propped open with the bootscraper. He made toast and tea, got out marmalade and butter. He stood eating, watching Gus guzzle his food then move slowly across the grass, cropping.

Hearing a car in the lane he hurried into the hall. Folly joined him. The car stopped by the gate; he heard voices. He looked out cautiously. The man he had seen prowling round the cottage was getting out of a police car. He slammed the door.

'Well, thanks, Constable. Thanks for listening anyway.'

'That's all right, Mr Jones. Any time.'

'I'll just tell Mrs Poliport.'

'You do that. You tell her. She and Mr Poliport were always interested I understand.'

'Oh yes, he was particularly.'

'A nice gentleman. Goodbye, Mr Jones. See you.'

'Goodbye.' The car drove off, footsteps came up the path. Hugh retreated up the stairs to the landing.

Gus honked.

'Hey, Gus, where's Matilda then?' The man came to the kitchen door, calling.

'Matilda, hey Matilda, where are you?' He thumped the back door, walked into the kitchen. Hugh slipped back into Matilda's room, caught up Folly into his arms and dived into her hanging cupboard, bending down, pushing between the coats and dresses to the back where he sat down on a heap of cushions.

Mr Jones moved noisily about downstairs, talking to himself and the gander.

'Where is she, then? I came early this morning. She wasn't here, boyo, not here to see Jones. There, there, don't honk so. You know me. You honked this morning but she's fed you since. Ah, kettle's hot. She's had her breakfast, not put away the butter nor the marmalade. Don't come in boy and make a mess, you know what she's like.'

There was a listening pause. 'Matilda? You ill or something, Matilda?' Then steps on the stairs. Mr Jones was coming up. Hugh held Folly's nose lightly.

'Matilda, you in there?' Steps in the room. 'Not made her bed. Funny. Gone out in a hurry.' The springs of the bed were bounced. 'My, what a comfortable bed she has.' Hugh held his breath. The cupboard door opened suddenly, letting in light. 'Not in there either. Hardly be hiding in her cupboard. Must look in the garage.' Then a loud shout as the footsteps retreated down the stairs. 'Matilda! I know I bore you woman, but there's no need to hide. I told you I won't do it again, I told you!' There was anger and pain in the voice, frustration. Mr Jones in the kitchen called for the last time.

'Matilda?'

Hugh crept out of the cupboard, keeping well out of sight, looked down on Mr Jones. Short, thickset, a forest of a beard, thin strands of hair trained over a large head from ear to ear. From Hugh's view-point the top of Mr Jones' head looked like spaghetti junction. He stood looking about him with one hand stroking the strands into place. Presently he moved off to the garage, his feet slapping on the stone path. Hugh heard him say, 'Gone out then. Where's she gone, Gus? Ah me, poor Jones, I should have known better. I should never have tried.' The gander honked and flapped dismissing wings. Mr Jones reached the gate. 'You tell her, boyo, I'll be back.' The gander resumed his cropping, unmoved by the rather affected Welsh voice. Hugh swore. Damn the man, when would he be coming back? Obviously he'd got a lech for Matilda. He tidied Matilda's bed. Fine thing if Jones had come in to find him in it. He sat on the edge of the bed considering what to do, idly thumbing through the book she must be reading at the moment. Rosamund Lehmann's *The Ballad and the Source* – notes in pencil on the flyleaf in Matilda's hand, but shaky:

I think only people like me do this. I get heightened perception. I'm insecure. I'm pissed on pot, Claud darling. I found it in his overcoat, him of all people! He made me safe. This perception is awful. I found it last night, I wonder if – no not last night – last year *Claud, it's made me remember* – it was at a party –

The writing straggled and stopped. Hugh sniffed the book. I'm not a trained Labrador, he thought. Then he remembered the overcoat at the back of Matilda's cupboard, crawled back in.

In the pockets of an overcoat he found a sizeable amount of cannabis and a packet of heroin. He flushed the heroin down the lavatory and pocketed the cannabis. It would be interesting to know why Matilda had left evidence of Tom while sweeping herself out of the house before her picnic. And the note to Claud? Perhaps Claud was the only one she could talk to. Hugh walked thoughtfully downstairs.

Mr Jones was standing in the kitchen.

'I thought there must be someone here,' he said. 'Who are you?'

'My name is Hugh Warner.'

'The Matricide, eh?'

'Yes.'

'Mine is Jones.'

'How d'you do.'

'Matilda usually asks me to care for Gus when she goes away.'

'I'm doing it.'

'Good.' Mr Jones looked hesitant. 'Do you know when she will be back?'

'No.'

'Oh.'

'I've just flushed the heroin down the loo –'

'Oh de-arr!'

'I suppose it comes in the UFOs.'

'Clever you are.'

'Matilda seems to have found out.'

'Oh de-arr.'

'Shall we ring the police separately or together?'

'Whatever for?'

'You can tell them about me and I can tell them about you.'

'No.'

'No?'

'Too upsetting for Matilda. When did she find out about Tom, then?'

'I don't know.'

'I bet she's strangled the knowledge.' Mr Jones teased his hair carefully. 'She does that, it's her gift. She won't remember anything she wishes to forget, if you catch the drift.'

'I've caught it.'

Mr Jones laughed.

'How much heroin was there?'

'One packet.'

'Good, that's what I missed. Ah well, not to worry. Since Tom's untimely heart attack all that's over.'

'But you reported a UFO this morning.'

'So you were listening? They don't come any more, not since Tom's demise. I just go on occasionally reporting one. You should never stop anything suddenly, it makes the police suspicious.' The Welsh accent had returned. Hugh began to laugh.

'Do you play chess?' asked Mr Jones. 'Tom was a very

103

good player. I miss it.'

Hugh nodded.

'Good. Did you sleep in her bed last night? It was warm when I felt it.'

'Yes.'

'In the cupboard were you?'

'Yes.'

'It would be nice to sleep in that bed with Matilda.'

'I hadn't thought of it.'

'But I have.' Mr Jones sighed. 'I suggested it. Fatal. She was offended. Took offence.'

'Poor Mr Jones.'

'Yes, poor Jones, poor Jones.'

'I suppose,' Mr Jones said later as he took his leave, 'you were missing your mother.'

Hugh made no reply.

'I was referring to your sleeping in Matilda's bed, obliquely of course. It is Freudian.'

'Of course.'

'And what do you know about UFOs?'

'Nothing.'

'Hah! Nothing he says. They came up the creek, a little sea-plane it is, was, I should say.'

'Where?'

'On the river. They cut out the engine and landed on the water. So easy it was.'

'Your idea?'

'No, no, man, Tom. Tom's idea, his organization, a sideline.'

'Well, I flushed it down the loo.'

'Couldn't flush your mother. Had to leave her on the sofa. That was messy.'

'Heroin's worse.'

'A point there. Do you mind the pot?'

'No, I'm not averse. I think it's harmless.'

'So is death. The newspaper said she could not have known much. It is you that do the knowing.'

'Oh, bugger off.'

'All right I will, but presently we can play chess and

share a joint while Matilda's away?'

'All right.' Hugh felt inclined to like Matilda's suitor. Heavily bearded, paunchy, squat, he had beautiful liquid black eyes.

Mr Jones walked crabwise along the path. 'I will bring my chessboard. It is nicer than Tom's. It was my Da's. The feel of the ivory is good to the fingers, engenders thought.'

'Goodoh.' Hugh was amused.

'And yesterday's paper. You were seen in Rome at the airport changing planes, it says. It says in the *Daily Mirror*, look you.'

'Jolly good, Dai Jones.'

'My name is not David, it is also Huw, but HUW not HUGH.' Mr Jones paused to let this sink in, then, 'Not to worry, it is the disappearing bride from the beach they are on about. The poor husband is frantic, naked she is, wandering.'

'Ah yes, I'd forgotten I had competition. What about the man who ate his wife's dog?'

'Ah that!' Mr Jones paused, one foot slightly airborne. 'That woman is clever, oh she is. She said the dog had rabies. The poor husband is in an isolation hospital having painful injections in his greedy stomach. He is under observation, look you, daren't take the risk.'

'Are you really Welsh?'

Mr Jones laughed. 'Never been there. Born in Tooting. It's the fashion, that's all. Gives me class.'

'Of course.'

'Not like Winchester and Oxbridge but it's cheaper to obtain.' Mr Jones reached the gate. 'See you for chess then.' The gate clicked shut and he was gone.

16

Matilda arrived in London in the early evening, taking a taxi to Chelsea. She put the window down so that she could hear and smell London, the roar of the traffic, heels clicking on pavements, engines revving as they waited for lights to change. The constant chat on the taxi radio, blare of musak from open shops, exclamations in foreign languages, people of many nations hurrying across before the lights changed. Just as she thought she could bear no more the taxi turned into John's cul-de-sac on the border of Chelsea and Fulham.

John came out to meet her, paid the taxi, took her case, bent to kiss her.

'Lovely to see you, Matty, absolutely great. Come in and have a drink.' He was using a new shaving lotion she noticed and was glad. Up to now he had used the same as Tom. She wondered whether this was tact or chance. He led her into his sitting-room. 'Sit down, Matty, you must be tired. What will you drink? Whisky? Vodka? Sherry? Gin? I'm drinking vodka, suits the weather. Vodka and tonic?'

'Yes please.' How like John to offer a choice but do the choosing.

'You've altered the room.' She accepted her vodka with a slice of lemon. He must have had that lemon sliced, she thought, doesn't want it wasted.

'Yes, do you like it? I've got this new sofa. I sold the old chairs. They fetched a very good price.'

'They were a bit rickety.' Matilda felt the need for assertion. This was London she had just sniffed, one must be sharp.

'Yes, need a bit spending on them. They've gone to America.'

'So much does.'

'So much does, yes. I've changed the house round a bit, hope you will like it. I sleep at the back now. The spare room is at the front.'

'Oh good, how clever of you. It must be almost like a new house.' Matilda sipped. 'What frightfully strong vodka. Might I have a little more tonic?'

John took her glass. There would be no memories of Tom in the new spare room, she thought, looking at John's back, so young for his age, such a good figure. She knew he did exercises. John poured in a little tonic. He wondered how much she still grieved for Tom.

'I thought we'd dine at home tonight and go out tomorrow, unless you have plans.' He handed back her glass.

'No plans. Dinner here will be lovely. I'd rather not be seen until I've had my hair done.'

'You look very nice, as always.'

'My hair looks like a chicken.' She could not say "Polish Fowl" and, as she withheld it, wondered why not.

'A ruffled hen.' John smiled. Goodness! Matilda thought, he is bland.

'You *know* you like your women well dressed. I shall have my hair done and wear a decent dress. I have a new one.' He wouldn't know she would be wearing a cast-off of Anabel's and shoes that had been Louise's.

'What are your plans?' John, sitting opposite, quizzed her. She wore well, he thought. He hoped the dress would be Anabel's as he didn't care for Louise's taste. The elder of Matilda's daughters dressed rather loudly. Anabel, whose very appearance was a call to bed, had the quieter dress sense.

'What are your plans?' he repeated.

'My hair, some shopping, any exhibitions I may fancy, nothing much, just a sniff of London.' As though searching for a handkerchief, Matilda felt in her bag for Hugh's key.

'I'll give you a latchkey. You must come and go as you please. Another drink?'

The man's got sixth sense, Matilda thought. Christ! I must be careful. 'No, no more. May I have a bath before dinner?'

'Of course. The supper is cold. Take your time. There's no hurry.'

Matilda looked at him. 'Dear John, it is good to see you and you look so well, such a marvellous figure.'

'Piers. I play squash. Try and remember Piers. And I garden –'

She went upstairs. He followed, carrying her case. 'I hope you will be comfortable.'

'I'm sure I shall.'

How stilted we are. He behaves as if he's being careful too. I must be crazy. Matilda turned on the bath, began unpacking, hanging Anabel's dress in the cupboard, throwing her nightdress on the bed, putting her few clothes away in the chest of drawers. She lay in the bath. I must be very careful, she thought. When I've used that key I'll post it back to myself at home. It was silly to be afraid of John but it would be sillier to risk anything. Better to humour him, call him Piers if that's what he wants.

At dinner John gave her a run-down of new books, plays, films, exhibitions, current affairs. The fishing season good on the Test in spite of the long dry spell, birds at Minsmere, mutual friends. Matilda listened, saying 'Yes?', 'No!', 'Oh really?', 'How extraordinary and how very interesting!' while she ate delicious iced cucumber soup, salmon mousse with a ratatouille, which she herself would not have served together, and mountain strawberries with Kirsch. She would have preferred them plain but exclaimed with delight over them. John's choice of wine was impeccable – a Niersteiner. She refused brandy, accepted coffee.

Without asking whether she minded, John turned on the radio to listen to a concert he wished to hear. She's not musical, she can put up with it, he thought. Matilda, who happened to know and like the particular symphony being played, listened until the end and, when he switched it off, remarked:

'I love that one, so much prefer it to the sixth, don't you?'

'Oh yes, the sixth is played far too often.' The bloody bitch, John thought, looking at Matilda's chin, slight and undecided. 'More coffee? A brandy now before bed?'

'No, Piers, no thank you. Have you been away?'

When she smiled the chin altered, stopped being weak. He wondered why, as he often had before, liking to know people exactly.

'I was going but then this Warner affair blew up. I shall go next week, it's a small delay that's all.'

'Where are you going?' Matilda kept her voice steady by refusing to hear the name Warner.

'Czechoslovakia.'

'Fishing?'

'No, no, this is work. The fellow is, it seems, in Prague, which complicates things slightly.'

'What fellow?' Her voice steady, lifting up her coffee cup, looking across at John/Piers the future knight.

'Hugh Warner, the man they call the Matricide. You must have read the papers. Killed his mother, smashed in her skull with a tea-tray.'

'Oh, of course,' Matilda hoped her heart could not be seen thundering against her ribcage. 'Of course I've read about him. I'm more amused though by the man who ate his wife's dog. He must be some sort of pervert, don't you think?' She put her cup down on the table beside her, triumphant when it did not rattle.

'He's not a pervert.'

'Oh John – to eat a dog!'

'I'm talking about Warner. The "ate wife's dog" man must have done it for publicity. No, I'm talking about Warner.'

'What's he to do with you?'

'The office is interested. The assassination of his mother was just a cover.'

'It must be very serious to have such a desperate cover.' Matilda affected eager interest. 'Tell me more – what's it about?'

'I can't, Matty.' She hated him calling her Matty. 'You should know by now I don't talk.'

'Another Burgess and Maclean? A Philby? They didn't murder their mothers, did they? Goodness me, reading the papers one would never guess.'

'Don't be silly, Matty. It's a sort of – let's call it a parallel.'

'Call it anything you like, Johnnie. How do you know he's in Prague?'

'I can't tell you that but he is. Why d'you call me Johnnie suddenly? You never have before. Call me Piers.'

'You call me Matty and I hate it. Are you going to Prague to see him?'

'I can't tell you that either. Don't pry, Matty. I shall call you Matty. I want to, I always have. It would be difficult to change now.'

'I'm sure I asked you not to. I must have.'

'No, no never.' John well remembered the occasion when she had, the intonation of her voice. It was all a long time ago but clear.

'It must have been someone else, then. What a fascinating life you lead. Off to Prague to meet the Matricide. Will you say "Boo" or will he?'

John laughed. 'Keep it under your hat.'

'Of course I shall.' What a comical old bugger he is, thought Matilda. This is a real Beclean filthy. 'The papers keep saying he's been seen in a new place every day but they haven't mentioned Prague yet. Why d'you think he went there?'

'I can't discuss it any more, Matilda. You know me.'

'I wonder whether I do. What did he do? What's his profession? The man who ate the dog is a builder.'

'I don't think there's any connection.' John got up and poured himself another brandy. How these London people put it away. Matilda shook her head when John made a mute offer.

'Just the Silly Season.' Matilda smiled. 'What was his profession?'

'He was in publishing, lived not far from here.' John mentioned the address Matilda had memorized, the house whose key lay in her bag.

'Oh really? Not a bad area now. It's grown quite smart. Our mothers thought it beyond the pale, poor old snobs. Have you been there?'

'Of course not. The police let my people have a look. Nothing to see, naturally.'

Matilda yawned, putting her hand up to her mouth. 'What an interesting job you have, absorbing,' repeating herself.

'Not bad.' John looked at her hand. Hands showed age more than faces. She was six months younger than he, or was it a year?

'I must go to bed.' Matilda stood up. 'A long day tomorrow.'

'Shall we meet here, then, for dinner?'

'Yes please.'

'Would you like to dine at Wheelers? They have oysters. I have rung them up.'

'Dear John, I should love it. Sorry – Piers.' Matilda held up her cheek to be kissed. 'Goodnight, bless you.'

John kissed the proffered cheek – quite hard, not flabby. 'Goodnight, bless you.'

'How easily we say "bless you". Do we mean it?'

'Of course we do, Matilda. What can you mean? One always blesses an old friend.'

'I was joking, Piers, joking.' Matilda went steadily up to bed, determined not to hurry. In her room she pulled the ribbon off the top of her nightdress and, stringing Hugh's key on it, wore it round her neck, pulling the duvet up to her chin. It was like John to have the most expensive duvet from Harrods. She missed the weight of sheets and blankets and, with a sudden pang, missed the pressure of a dog in the small of her back. She must not think of Stub, it was weakening.

Sleep did not come easily. She listened to John

111

moving about downstairs, locking and double-locking the front door, bolting the windows. If there were a fire, she thought, we'd never get out. The key lay heavy between her breasts. Hearing John's footsteps on the stairs, she held it tight in her hand.

'You all right, old girl? Got everything you want?' he called from the landing.

'Yes, thank you. Lovely new duvet.'

'Harrods. Sleep well.'

'Thanks, same to you.' She turned on her side, away from the window, disturbed by the light from the street lamp. For what seemed hours she lay wakeful, worrying. Would Hugh be careful – keep out of sight? Would Gus be safe? The dog? Had she forgotten anything? The unaccustomed rich food was taking its time settling in her stomach. She got up and tiptoed to the window. It only opened a little way, not enough for even a thin burglar to climb through. She knelt down and breathed the street air, listening to the roar of the city which never quietened.

In childhood she had listened from her grandparents' house, heard trains shrieking in the distance, tugs tooting on the river, taxi doors slamming, the creak of cowls on chimney pots as they whirled in the wind, turning this way and that like the heads of armoured knights. The Clean Air Act had put paid to them. She remembered, too, how once when she was very small she had heard sheep and seen a flock driven through her grandparents' square to Hyde Park. She wanted to remember that dawn, was comforted that she did. I will get his money tomorrow, she thought, and then forget all about him while I am here. She fell asleep, holding the latchkey in her hand, her mouth open, snoring.

Across the landing John, roused by his bladder, stood in his bathroom. He thought crossly that in youth he would have lasted the night. Then he cocked his head. God almighty, how she snores. Nothing wrong with my hearing anyway. How could Tom have put up with it all those years? A bit uppity calling him 'Johnnie'.

Menopausal cheek, must make allowances. She'd seemed a bit edgy somehow, something on her mind. Probably still missing Tom. It had been a pity, that heart attack.

17

In the morning Matilda sat in bed eating breakfast brought up by John's housekeeper. Mrs Green was a woman who while modern in appearance could create a Mrs Tiggywinkle atmosphere if she so wished. The tray placed across Matilda's knees held coffee, boiled eggs, toast, butter, marmalade and a linen napkin.

'It's lovely to see you. It's ages, isn't it? You are spoiling me.'

'Far too long, Madam.' Matilda knew well that the 'Madam' bit was a joke, that she was referred to by her Christian name behind her back.

'This is delicious. Dinner last night was a dream.'

'I'm glad you liked it.' Mrs Green smoothed Matilda's duvet. 'He would have the ratatouille with the mousse, said it had to be eaten up. Getting a trifle mean, our Mr Leach, doesn't like anything wasted.'

'It was a very good ratatouille.'

'I just thought I'd mention it. I wouldn't like you to think it was my idea.'

Matilda crunched her toast, poured coffee, topped her eggs. There was more to come.

'It's his age, Madam.'

Matilda raised an eyebrow, glanced at Mrs Green.

'The male menopause, Madam.'

'Go on –'

'True, Madam, Mr Green has it too.'

'Wow!'

'Of course Mr Poliport wouldn't have –'

'Didn't live to have it, Mrs Green.'

'Oh, Madam.'

'Don't let's think about it.'

'No, Madam, of course not. But I just thought I'd mention it in case Mr Leach seemed a bit funny.'

'No funnier than usual.'

'Oh good. Of course I took Mr Green to the doctor. He takes pills now. That settles him.'

'Female hormones?'

'Oh, you know about them.' Mrs Green was disappointed.

'I don't really think Mr Leach needs pills, not yet anyway. But he's got you to keep an eye on him, lucky fellow.' She could see that Mrs Green also considered John fortunate.

'Would Madam like the telephone? I can plug it in for you.'

'Oh, I would. I've got to do something about my hair.'

'I took a chance. I made an appointment for you at Paul's for eleven.'

'Mrs Green, I could kiss you.'

'Also your friends Lalage and Anne are in London, but Mrs Lucas and Mrs Stern are away, Madam.'

'You've been spying for me!'

'Anticipating your desires, Madam.'

'Stop the "Madam", Mrs Green. You know you call me Matilda to your husband and everyone else.'

Mrs Green laughed. 'I'll get the telephone. D'you want your dress for tonight pressed?'

'No, it's that black thing of Anabel's. D'you think I shall look all right in it?'

'If Anabel does, you will. You are the same size.'

'Have you seen Anabel lately?'

'No,' said Mrs Green, who had, and thought Anabel a selfish good-for-nothing tart to neglect her mother so.

'Nor have I. She seems to like living in Germany.'

Mrs Green made a non-committal noise and went to fetch the telephone. 'Don't be late for your appointment. You know that Paul –'

'All right, I won't.' Matilda telephoned Lalage.

'Lalage? It's me. Lunch tomorrow?'

'La Green warned me,' shrieked the telephone voice. 'Of course, sweetie, lunch tomorrow. Come here. Anne left a message. Lunch with her the day after tomorrow. La Green rang her up. All right?'

'Sure.'

'See you tomorrow, must rush. I'm having my face done, late already, 'bye.'

'She's having her face done, Mrs Green.'

'Wait till you see it.' Mrs Green showed her teeth.

'Oh, Mrs Green, up again? Really?'

'Yes. Cost a thousand, I believe. Her husband's made of money – diamonds – a new car too.'

'None of that envy now. I must get up. I have to see to my hair. Just look at it.'

'Her hair is blonde now.'

'Thank you for warning me. What's Anne's?'

'Same old red.'

'Ah.'

'You keep yours as it is.'

'I shall, I shall. Can't do anything else in the country even if I wanted to.'

Matilda put on her frock, several years old but date-less. She had bought it with Anabel's help for Tom's funeral. She had barely looked at the garment when Anabel had taken her to buy it, her mind had been full of the horror of meeting the plane carrying Tom's coffin. The coffin had lain in the sitting-room for the time it had taken to arrange the cremation, buy the dress, wait for Louise, Mark and Claud to arrive. Louise had said:

'Why here, for God's sake, Mother? Why can't it be in the crematorium chapel?'

'I want it here. He would be lonely in the chapel, out of place. He had no beliefs.' Then Claud had said, 'Shut up,' to Louise, and Mark, who agreed with her, had shut up too. Matilda zipped up the dress.

'Do I look respectable?' she asked Mrs Green.

'Very chick.' Mrs Green pronounced her 'chic' as in

116

Chicago. She had heard Matilda say this when younger, happier.

'It's not new. I'm mean about clothes. I live in jeans in the country.'

'You look fine.' Mrs Green watched Matilda go out into the street. 'Don't let that Paul ruin your hair.'

'I won't.'

Matilda caught a bus, rocked and roared along the King's Road, up Sloane Street, lurching round into Knightsbridge, grinding up to Piccadilly. She walked through side streets to Paul's.

The silence as she went into the hairdresser's was a relief after the racket in the street. Paul met her.

'Hello, Paul.'

'I've got a job ahead of me I see. Evie, shampoo Mrs Poliport then bring her to me. Just got to cut a slice off a Frog visitor then I'll be with you.'

'She'll hear you, Paul.'

'What if she does? These Frogs and Krauts only come once or twice. It doesn't pay to bother, I haven't the time.'

'He doesn't change, does he?'

Matilda submitted to a brisk shampoo, feeling relief when Evie finished and turbanned her head in a towel.

'Now what have we got here?' In disgust Paul flicked Matilda's wet hair upwards. 'Who cut it last? Been nibbled by a mouse?'

'You cut it.'

'Never.'

'You did, when you came to do that demonstration at the Grand Hotel.'

'Oh, I remember. It wasn't my day. Robert and I had had a row.'

'Be more careful this time. I hope you haven't had a row lately.'

'We split up. I'm ever so peaceful now, living with a gloomy Dane.'

'Good news.'

'Wouldn't you like a rinse?'

'No, I wouldn't.'

'All your friends have them. Needn't be red, you know. Just a bit of gold in with the silver. It would suit you.'

'No thanks.'

'Honestly? Why not tart you up a bit?'

'Honestly, Paul, leave it alone.'

'How right you are. All the old Fraus look years older than you, your hair looks terribly distinguished with your skin. How do you do it?'

'Come on, Paul. Concentrate. Snip, snip, but don't get carried away.'

'Very well.' Paul's tired eyes met Matilda's in the glass. 'I'll take great care. You don't come often but I'm glad when you do.'

'What a nice thing to say.' Paul snipped, concentrating, combing her hair this way and that, snipping off tiny bits, the scissors, razor sharp, flickering between his fingers.

'Have you seen Anabel or Louise lately?'

'No, Paul. I think they have their hair done abroad. They haven't been over for ages.'

'No.' Paul, who had cut Anabel's hair a few days before, agreed. 'They've got lovely hair like you, though I don't think either of them will go your colour.'

'Why not?'

'All those rinses. Girls forget the colour they were born with. Very few white heads these days. There, how's that? Suits your head.' He held a mirror so that she could see. 'Janey, blow Mrs Poliport then bring her back to me.'

Janey led Matilda away and brushed and blew.

'That's better.' Paul gave a final snip or two. 'Be all right now.'

'Thank you. I feel ready to face the world.'

'See you soon?'

'I don't know when I shall be in London again, if ever.'

'Goodbye then –' Paul was already hurrying to another customer. Matilda was forgotten. She paid the astronomical sum asked, tipped the girls, walked downstairs into the street, strolling slowly along to Green Park Tube.

As she went down the steps the hot air blowing up from below lifted her new hair and blew it every which way.

She bought a ticket to Gloucester Road and went down into the bowels of London. It was time to find Hugh's money. She wanted the job over, behind her, so that she could forget it.

Sitting in the train, which was bursting with young foreigners carrying parcels, shouting to one another above the noise of the train, Matilda breathed deeply to calm her nerves and repeated Hugh's instructions to herself to be sure she had them right. She got out at Gloucester Road and walked to Hugh's flat. Long before she rounded the corner into the Gardens she had his keys in her hand, one for the street door, the other for the flat.

The police would no longer be watching the flat but John's fantasies of the night before made her nervous. If there were suspicious-looking people in the street she would walk past the house. But who was or was not suspicious? The few people about looked ordinary enough. When she reached the house she fitted the key in the door, opened the door and walked in.

The hall was dark and drab, the stairs steep and badly carpeted. She counted them as she made a slow ascent – eighty-five, eighty-six, eighty-seven. Eighty-seven brought her to the small landing and the door which still had a card by the bell which said 'Hugh Warner'.

Matilda listened.

No sound. Nobody coming up or going down. Hugh had said that nearly everyone in the house went out to work all day every day. She ran her finger under the left hand edge of the landing carpet and found the string. He didn't lie about this, she thought. She pulled. From under the carpet came the envelope. She put it in her bag. Two steps down in the fold of carpet over the step another string brought a second envelope. Two steps more, another tweak and she had the rest of the money. She was breathing hard. Should she or should she not go into the flat? It was not really necessary; he could manage without shoes. Curiosity won. She let herself in quickly,

119

closing the door behind her. The flat looked undisturbed though there had been a search by the police. She did not believe in John's Beclean filthy people.

She looked curiously round Hugh's home. Books. He was considerably more erudite than he appeared. Some good pictures. A stack of records, a very nice record player. A bathroom she envied. She looked wistfully at a Greek sponge, decided to leave it. Clothes she must leave too. The bedroom was comfortable. She felt the big bed gingerly. The flat was friendly. A snapshot of a woman smiling at the camera from a garden chair, a black cat in her arms – unmistakably his mother, the nose feminine but large. 'Well, Mother.' Matilda looked at this version of Hugh. 'You were not afraid that day.' In the street a car door slammed. She heard voices, the insertion of a key in the front door. She looked around for a hiding place, moving out of sight of the door. Footsteps pounding up the stairs, a man and a girl talking.

'My God, what stairs! How much further? My legs ache.'

'Top floor, I'm afraid.'

'Ooh!' in a squeak. 'You didn't say the Matricide lived here.'

'I did, stupid, you were too pissed to hear. Come on.'

'It's scary.'

'Don't be stupid. He isn't in there.'

The footsteps went on up the stairs. Matilda let out her breath. She snatched up a pair of shoes from the rack, let herself out of the flat and ran down to the street. In Gloucester road she bought a carrier bag and put the shoes in it. The shop girl looked at her briefly, then away to the next customer while she held out her hand with the change.

She asked in a fruit shop where the nearest post office would be and walked steadily along the pavement towards it. She was sweating with retrospective fear. Her feet hurt in their thin soles on the London pavements. She hoped she looked unobtrusive among the throng of foreigners pushing and barging towards the tube.

'Qu'est-ce qu'elle fait ces jours-ci, Madeleine?'

'Il paraît qu'elle fait le trottoir.'

'C'est pas vrai. Elle ne s'est donc pas mise avec un Suisse?'

'Comme elle doit se barber!'

Perhaps Madeleine's feet had hurt on the trottoir? Matilda pushed into the post office, joined a queue edging slowly towards the counter. Her feet swelling unbearably, she waited, holding Hugh's keys in her hand. As she moved slowly up the queue she took the keys off her nightdress ribbon, putting the ribbon back in her bag. When at last she reached the counter she found herself face to face with an Indian, whose sad eyes looked through her.

'A registered envelope please, medium size.'

Delicate fingers pushed the envelope towards her. She paid. He would not know her again, this man imprisoned behind the counter, so infinitely more dignified than nose-picking Mr Hicks. Mr Hicks feeling superior with his itchy nose and putty-coloured skin would call him a nig-nog or coon.

'Next please.' The Indian waved three fingers just a trifle. She was holding up the queue staring.

'Sorry.' Matilda blushed, hurried to a counter and addressed the envelope to herself, put in the keys, first wrapping them in a telegraph form, licked up the envelope, closed it firmly, pressing hard, then posted it. Overwhelmed with relief she went out to the street and waited to take a taxi which was disgorging some Arab ladies outside an hotel. After giving John's address she sat back, easing her feet from their tight shoes.

That evening at Wheelers she greedily ate a dozen oysters and a sole and listened with pleasure to John's description of a day's fishing on the Test, conscious that with her hair properly cut she looked more than presentable in Anabel's dress and glad that Louise took shoes a size larger than she did.

'London pavements are death to my feet, John dear, does it show in my face – Piers, I mean.'

'You look younger than I've seen you look since Tom

121

died, if I may say so. You look splendid, Matty. What are you doing these days?'

'Just living, John – Piers.'

'It's been very hard for you, you two were so close.'

'Dreadfully. I wished for a long time to be dead, in fact I wish it still.'

'The children should be considered.'

'Louise, Mark, Anabel and Claud have their own lives.'

'They come and see you.'

'No. One visit each after the funeral, then away they went.'

'I should have thought –'

'None of them lives in England. They are all busy people.'

'Do you go to see them?'

'I haven't so far.'

'Really? It's three years since Tom died. I should have thought –'

'I don't particularly want to go. The States are so far. I hate Paris. I don't like Frankfurt either.'

'Tom liked Paris.'

'I never went with him.'

'Yes, I know that.'

'How?' Matilda asked sharply. 'How did you know? We were pretty well inseparable.'

'I suppose he told me. Yes, yes that must have been it.' John looked slyly at Matilda. 'There's no harm in telling you now. I knew you never went with him. He told me so, naturally.'

'What do you mean, naturally?'

'Tom used to do little jobs for my department. They paid for his trips.'

Matilda flushed. 'John, you go too far with your fantasies. Don't start telling me Tom was a spy. It's too bad of you.'

'My dear girl –'

'I'm not a girl, yours or anybody else's. I'm too old to play silly spy games with you. It used to be funny, but

122

bringing Tom in like this isn't: It's indecent, it's worse than rotten taste.'

'I'm sorry if I –'

'I should hope so. We laughed at you over Burgess and Maclean, and Philby and you made me laugh last night over your date in Prague with the man who murdered his mother.' Matilda prevented herself from saying 'Hugh'. 'But I tell you, John, it's not funny when you insinuate Tom was a sort of agent; it's revolting.'

'Sorry, my dear. It's a foible. Forgive me.' John signalled to the waiter to bring his bill, looking away from Matilda, pleased to find she knew nothing, suspected nothing. He had not been sure these three years that Matilda believed in Tom's heart attack. It had been unfortunate. Nice to make sure of Matilda's ignorance. They had been close, those two.

Matilda watched John pay the bill and thought, the cost of this meal would keep ten third world families going for months. She was still angry.

'It's a dangerous foible, John, and hurtful.'

'I apologize, Matty, I am truly sorry. How can I make amends? Tell you I am not going to Prague to meet this mother-murderer, that I'm only going for the fishing?'

Matilda looked at him doubtfully. She had enjoyed the Prague fantasy; it had made her feel safe.

'I don't think you know truth from fiction and it doesn't matter but you should be more careful. You hurt me.'

'Matty, I am sorry. Shall we go? Finish the apologies.'

'Let's walk a little. I'll tell you a secret. I'm wearing a pair of Louise's shoes. My feet swell on these pavements.'

John took her arm and said cheerfully, 'And I will tell you one too. I sleep with a revolver under my pillow – always have.'

Matilda burst out laughing. John laughed too, though he was still a little annoyed with what he considered her prissy reaction over Tom. 'I showed it to Tom on one occasion and he said, "Never tell Matty, it would scare the pants off her." '

'He never called me Matty.'

'No, of course he didn't.'

'And I don't believe in the revolver.'

'There is no need for you to.'

Matilda thought this answer ambiguous and decided to cut short her visit. London suddenly seemed too large, too noisy, too much for her altogether. Too much for her feet.

'I shall have to go home very soon.'

'You've only just arrived.'

'There's nothing for me in London, John, not any more. Piers, if you like.'

'It's lovely to see you. Don't hurry away now you're here.'

'It's such a pity there's no fishing near me. Wouldn't it be nice if there were?'

She's taken offence, thought John. No matter, she's saved herself a heart attack which would be boring for me to arrange. I don't want to stay with her anyway.

'When must you go?'

'In a couple of days, if I may stay that long.'

'You know you may. I'm not going to Prague until Saturday. Today is Tuesday.'

'I shall go on Thursday then.'

'Why don't you ring up?'

'There is nobody to ring up. I live solo.'

'Yes, of course.'

'Don't advise me to marry again.'

'I wouldn't dream of it.'

'Louise, Mark, Anabel and Claud have.'

'Fools.'

'And you're an angel.'

'With foibles.' They had reached John's house and he reached for his key. 'A nightcap? Brandy?'

'No. Bed for me. Thank you, I've had a lovely evening.' Matilda left him and later in bed wondered whether he did or did not sleep with a revolver under his pillow. She felt anxious and disturbed, wishing she were at home.

In his room John read for a while, checked that his

revolver was correctly placed before turning off the bedside lamp. He lay smiling. Matilda was splendidly naïve. He thought and wondered, without being more than mildly amused, what sort of fellow she was shacked up with and why she should be toting his shoes around in a carrier bag. Larger feet than Tom's, not Mark's or Claud's style. It was probably somebody quite unpresentable. He switched his mind to his trip to Prague. There were various conundrums which might be clearer after a night's sleep. It was aggravating that he had to do so many little jobs himself. Tom Poliport had proved irreplaceable, small cog though he had been.

Restless and unable to sleep, Matilda remembered Hugh's shoes. She had left the carrier bag in the hall. My Christ! What stupidity, she thought, tiptoeing down to fetch them. What a daft thing to do, though Mrs Green would not be in until morning.

18

Matilda was in good spirits at breakfast. John put his head round the door.

'Dinner tonight?'

'Yes, looking forward to it, Piers.'

'What are you doing today?'

'Lunching with Lalage. Some shopping. We won't lunch till late, knowing her.'

'Give her my regards.'

'I will.'

Later she set off, taking a quick look round Habitat and Peter Jones before taking a bus to Piccadilly. She crossed the street, looked in at Hatchard's on her way to what Tom called 'St Fortnum's, Piccadilly'. They had bought one another presents there when courting but today the memory did not bother her. She had discarded yesterday's high-heeled shoes and strode along in espadrilles. She bought a paté for Claud, arranging to have it sent to his New York apartment. The salesman gave her a card on which she wrote: *Eat this in memory of me. Mama.* He would eat it with his lover if it had not gone bad, which she rather hoped it would. She paid by cheque.

A short step into Jermyn Street, The careful choosing of a shirt for Louise at Turnbull and Asser. Louise would prefer something else and lend it to her husband whose colouring would be better suited to the shirt than Louise's. Matilda knew Louise would wonder whether her mother had chosen the shirt with this in view and tell herself her mother was not sophisticated enough to do anything so mean. She paid by cheque and had it sent to Paris.

She walked briskly to Liberty's where she chose two scarves for Anabel to match her most frequent moods, lust and satiation. Anabel would know what was meant. Here too she paid by cheque. A taxi to Foyle's where she bought the latest Russian poet in translation who had defected to the West and had it sent to Mark who would put it on his coffee table. She paid by cheque.

The shopping elevated her spirits to the necessary pitch to meet Lalage with a fair degree of calm, arriving for lunch a calculated ten minutes late.

'Darling, you are late! What on earth have you got on your feet?' Lalage kissed the side of Matilda's face, managing to look her over from head to foot. 'Darling, come in. I see you've been to Paul's. His prices are getting more astronomical every week.'

'Pretty steep,' Matilda agreed. 'How does it feel to be blonde then?'

'Oh sweetie, it's my natural colour. You must remember that. Your father used to call me Blondie.'

'That 'thirties cartoon?'

'Don't be naughty. Come in and tell all.'

Over lunch Matilda listened. Lalage chattered, her mouth full, about herself. In the time spent on drinks and the first course she told Matilda in immense detail about her face lift, each stitch, each pleat, and the price.

'I thought after the last lot you would not need to have it done again. That's what you said.'

'It didn't work out that way. I had a gallop. Swear you won't tell? It got damaged.'

'Who should I tell?'

'You might tell John, you're staying with him.'

'I won't if you don't want me to.'

'I don't mind really. It's just who I had the gallop with. After what he did my face fell so I had to have it pulled up again.'

'Who was the galloping Major then?'

'Not the Major, sweetie, the brother. The one who

127

killed his mother. You must know him – Warner.'

Matilda swallowed her soup and laughed.

'Lalage, come off it. He murdered his mother four weeks ago. You can't have been sleeping with him, had your face done and recovered in that short time.'

'You've got your dates mixed. How do you know, anyway?' Lalage, her expression limited by the amount of slack taken in, managed to look cross.

'I read the papers, watch the box, listen to the radio.'

Lalage, not put out, grinned. 'I'll use that one in a few months. All right, it was someone else. I did meet Hugh Warner once. I thought him very dishy. The huge nose is so sexy. Have you ever met him? His brother's a bit of a bore.'

'I don't think so.'

'I fear he's dead, must be or he would have been caught.'

'They don't catch them all.' Matilda was pleased by the steadiness of her voice. 'They never caught Jack the Ripper.'

'Well, he went for tarts, that was different. I don't suppose they really bothered. One's mother is different.'

Matilda grunted. 'Who were you galloping with then?'

'Ah, he's at the German embassy. He knows Anabel.' Lalage's glance was barbed.

'Lots of people know Anabel. She hasn't necessarily slept with them. She isn't a tart.'

'Steady on, love, I never said she was.'

'You implied by voice.'

'No, darling, no. Anabel's lovely. She gets around a lot. She's so pretty people are bound to talk about her. It's a pity about her hair.'

'She's young, it doesn't matter what she does to her hair.' How fast, Matilda thought sadly, one catches the breeze. What am I doing here talking to this spiteful old bag, she isn't my friend at all.

'I always loved Tom's hair, the way it flopped forward.' Lalage was removing their plates, fetching the next course. 'The same colour as Anabel's exactly, wasn't it?'

Lalage had her back to Matilda who sat forcing herself to be quiet, forcing herself not to get up and hit that freshly lifted face that knew that Tom's hair only flopped forward when he bent over making love. Then it flopped, but at no other time. She was surprised how mild her feelings were at having what had been a suspicion verified. So what? If he had slept with Lalage it didn't matter. Once she would have tried to kill Lalage; now she would not even slap her.

They finished the meal to the tune of Lalage's other affairs, her new fur coat, her new car, a hoped for diamond. As she combed her hair in Lalage's bedroom Matilda, her feet comfortable in their espadrilles, was able to say with easy laughter:

'Everything new, darling, face, clothes, car, lovers, everything except old moneybags. You are so clever to hang on to him.'

'My husband's not just an old moneybags, Matilda. You are a bitch.'

'Yes, I know. Thanks for the lunch. Take care of yourself. Give him my love. I suppose he's a veritable Kojak by now, poor Bertie.'

Matilda crossed Oxford Street and walked down to the Curzon cinema where there was an erotic German film showing. As she settled in her seat she thought idly, Tom must have been sloshed to sleep with Lalage. There was no doubt in her mind that he had. She was surprised she did not care. She dozed off after the first half of the film, took a taxi back to John's house, soaked agreeably in a boiling bath before dressing to go out. If Tom had slept with her friends then life was a little diminished. Time to go, time for the picnic.

'Would you like to have dinner at the Mirabelle or The Connaught?' John's voice called from the landing.

'You choose John, Piers I mean.'

'The Mirabelle then, and The Connaught tomorrow.'

'You spoil me.' Matilda ran more water in the bath. Staying with John was like having a rich, undemanding husband, though perhaps as a husband he might have demanded more? Somewhere at the back of her mind Matilda knew what he would demand. She decided to entertain him during dinner with a spiced up version of lunch at Lalage's.

John surprised her by taking her to a concert at the Festival Hall before dinner.

'You can rest your tootsies while I listen to music.'

'I do like music too you know –'

'You never used to.' He drove well, nosing his car easily through the traffic.

'Since Tom's death I've listened a lot to the radio. One can't help getting to know, recognize, love music.'

'Very bad for your ear unless you have a really good radio.'

'I haven't. All the same I've learned some music and a lot about current affairs. Sometimes I listen all day, it helps me.'

'Helps what?' John was parking the car, hoping Matilda wouldn't drop off during the concert.

'Helps me keep alive while I must.'

'Of course you must. You are not a suicidal character.'

That's what he thinks, poor old sod. Matilda was glad the concert was to be Mozart, a great cheerer-upper. Beethoven, John's favourite, was inclined to depress. She did not wish to drip tears onto Anabel's frock. She annoyed John by sitting alert and upright through the concert without nodding her head or toe-tapping, making several knowledgeable and intuitive remarks about the conductor. When at the end she turned and gave him a huge smile of thanks he was astonished to find how touchingly like she was to the Matilda he had known before her marriage. Driving her to the restaurant he felt kind and indulgent. She wasn't bad company; certainly tonight she looked presentable.

Eating dinner Matilda told John what Lalage had said or hinted about Anabel.

'She's like that, I shouldn't pay any attention. She's jealous of you, that's all.'

130

'Jealous of me?'

'Yes. Poor Bertie is the dreariest of bores. No wonder her face falls and has to be lifted.'

'But so rich.'

'I grant you that. He's disgustingly rich, does nothing interesting with it, just makes more money for Lalage to spend.'

'No need for her to pick on Anabel. How could she be sleeping with this German when he's in London and she's in Frankfurt?'

'There's that modern invention the aeroplane.'

'So it's true, then?'

'What if it was?' John, having seen Anabel with the German quite frequently, was not prepared to deny.

'I shouldn't mind.' Matilda looked around the restaurant. 'She's a beautiful girl. For aught I know she sleeps around a lot. She should be here, not me, it's a good setting for her. I don't belong anymore. The pavements are a disaster to my feet and I feel out of place. Anabel belongs, I don't.'

'Did Lalage suggest she had slept with Tom?'

'No,' said Matilda, too quickly, reinforcing John's knowledge.

'Have a brandy?'

'No, thank you, it would keep me awake.'

'Did you sleep well last night?'

Matilda wondered whether he had heard her creeping down for Hugh's shoes. 'Oh, I always use Claud's cure if I can't sleep.'

'What's that?'

'Composing letters to The Times about the Queen's hats. You have to write a letter which is not derogatory to the Monarchy but expresses your distaste for her headgear. Without appearing unpatriotic it's not possible. In despair you drop off and snore.' Matilda laughed as John grinned at her.

'Sure you won't have a brandy? D'you mind if I do?'

'Of course not. A brandy will suit you sitting there in your super pin-stripe. The onslaught of years has made

131

you very distinguished, Piers.' Matilda liked serving the occasional flattery.

'You are looking very pretty yourself.'

'It's the brief whiff of London you are treating me to.'

'Stay longer. Aren't you lonely in your cottage all on your own?'

'I've got a dog and a gander. I am a country bumpkin.'

'But not a lonely one?' She's being very secretive about this chap, John thought as he ordered brandy. I expect he's good in bed but drops his aitches.

'Not lonely at all. I won't mind going home on Thursday.'

He must be good, thought John. When I have the time I must find out who he is.

What a boring conversation this is. I prefer Gus any day. Matilda swallowed a yawn. It was long past her bedtime.

'You used to have a cat.'

'She died.'

'I'm sorry.'

'No use being sorry. Death is death. Tom's dead and our cat's dead. It won't be long before I'm dead too. Most of me died when Tom died. We had planned to die together.'

'Death control.'

'Yes. Did Tom tell you?'

'He must have. He wanted to go while the going was good. He got his wish.' John sniffed his brandy. If Tom had wished to die young the heart attack in the rue Jacob was really of little consequence. If I felt guilty which I don't, thought John, I should have no need to.

'Well, it was our wish. I got left. It's bloody hell,' Matilda snapped, anger making her look rather beautiful.

Whoever fits those shoes is lucky, if you like that sort of thing, which I happen to know she does. John watched her colour rise, pleased that Matilda believed in the heart attack, that there was no need to arrange one for her.

'You and Anabel are very alike.' He swallowed the brandy.

'Anabel and I? Goodness no.'

'Not in looks perhaps. Sexually.'

'What an extraordinary –' Matilda paused.

'Accusation?'

'Yes. I never slept around.'

'You might very easily have gone that way if Tom had let you out of his sight.'

Matilda let that pass, relieved that John was about to pay the bill.

'I'm lunching with Anne tomorrow. I wonder what she will have to say.'

'She will pick on Louise, you had Anabel today. Louise is also very beautiful, though not as sexy.'

'I shall try and be ready for her.'

'I'd let the girls protect themselves if they were mine.'

But they are not, thought Matilda, feeling sorry for John, unmarried, childless, sexless. What did he do on long winter evenings?

'You are an enigma,' she said later when she kissed his cheek goodnight. John felt complimented but not pleased and before going to bed checked his engagement diary and was annoyed to find there was no way of getting down to see Matilda until November. Big Feet must wait, he thought, switching off the light, feeling for his revolver.

In her room Matilda was not composing letters to The Times but congratulating herself on the fact that by the time the cheques she had written that day had bounced she would be dead. Let Mark worry. It would do him good to feel he had always been right in his opinion of his parents as unworldly, feckless people. As for her host John, if he had thought earlier of calling himself Piers a feast of confusion and derision would have been lost to anyone interested in her entourage, such as Claud. Matilda liked the words 'interested in her entourage' and mulled them over gently before snoring.

Listening to the snores, John lay thinking about

Matilda, remembering their youth. It had been too late to hold her, even if he had wanted to, when she had come running to him after killing Felicity. He had been glad she had killed Felicity, who was a nuisance. Desperate Matilda, so upset so long ago. 'I was so frightened I peed in the snow. It was so cold –' She had minded the cold more than killing. He had made her drink brandy, taken her along to Tom. And now, he thought, she's past fifty and snores like the devil.

19

On her way to lunch with Anne, Matilda strolled from Chelsea to Harrods. It had occurred to her to surprise Anabel by leaving a really beautiful dress worn only once. She would choose a dress which would suit both Anabel and Louise. They would find it, be aware of its cost, both want it. They would quarrel over who should have it. Anabel, the more ruthless and determined, would get it. Adrenaline would flow, brisk up the funeral. Later Louise would make her husband buy her an even more expensive dress and the anger would spread to him while Mark, who by this time would have visited the bank manager, would be furious. Only Claud would be delighted. Of all my children I love Claud the best, Matilda thought, as she walked into Harrods by the Hans Place entrance and strolled through the men's department to the lifts.

She enjoyed trying on and making up her mind. She was helped by an assistant who was not yet unkind to middle-aged ladies. Matilda confided that the dress was to be for Anabel after she had worn it once.

'I shall wear it tonight, then my daughter can have it.'

Matilda decided against white or black, havered a bit over a lime green which would suit Anabel but looked distressing with her white hair.

'There is a deep rose which would suit you.'

'Let me see it.'

The rose dress did suit. 'I shall have it. Anabel will look marvellous in it.'

'What about the length?' Matilda was wearing her

espadrilles. 'It will be rather short with heels.'

'I loathe heels, they hurt. I'm wearing these things to save pain. What shall I do?' She was distressed. She wanted the dress. With heels it would look ridiculous, too short.

'If you tried in the shoe department you might find a pair of dancing shoes. They are quite flat. I wear them often after a long day at work. My feet swell.'

'Do they at your age?'

'Yes.'

'Shall I go at once and find out, then come back if successful and pay for the dress?'

'Of course, Madam.'

'Will you take a cheque?'

'Of course.'

Successful with the dancing shoes, Matilda left Harrods carrying the dress and shoes, light in heart and lighter by one cheque for several hundred pounds. She walked through Montpelier Square to the park on her way to Anne in Mayfair.

Strolling along by the Serpentine she passed the spot where long ago she had biffed Felicity out onto the ice to her death without even the vaguest recollection of the event. She was filled with the euphoria of spending money she had not got. She enjoyed the crowds of young people walking, sitting, lying on the grass, in one case openly copulating. She liked the boats, ducks, prams, small children running. She enjoyed the shouting and screaming from the Lido, the flying of kites, orange, blue, red and green kites soaring and swooping in the late summer sky, reminding her for a moment of the blue sail she had seen on the sea during her abortive picnic. Next time she would surely be alone.

Anne lived in Mayfair; not for her Chelsea or Kensington. It was known that if she had consented to move to one of these areas her husband would have taken her on more holidays, given her a cottage in the country.

'I can only live in Mayfair, nowhere else,' had been

her cry. 'It's so near the shops.' It was said she could be seen shopping in street markets as far away as Lambeth, wearing black glasses and a headscarf – a rumour unconfirmed.

'Lovely to see you, darling.' Anne kissed Matilda. 'What have you got on your feet, for heaven's sake?'

'Espadrilles.'

'Darling, you can't be seen like that, people will laugh.'

'Suppose they do?'

'Oh, you've been *shopping*! Let's have a peep.' Anne's voice was the tone of a daily communicant who has caught a lapsed friend coming out of Mass. It combined surprise with forgiveness. Matilda showed her the dress and dancing slippers.

'It's not you, you know, is it the new mode? Those baby shoes?'

'Yes. I lunched with Lalage yesterday.'

'Darling, she mostly talks about her face you know.'

'I noticed. How is the family?'

'All right. Peter's in Greece, Humphrey is sailing. So boring, and death to one's hair. He always asks me to go too but it's not on, is it?'

'Why not?'

'Well, one feels sick, one gets bored, one's hair goes the most dreadful carrot, you know, and it's difficult to get back to normal, you know.'

'How would I know?'

'Well, love, you can wear it white but at this moment in time one can't, you know.'

'How is Vanessa?'

'Vanessa has some dreadful man in your part of the world. You probably know him, Bobby something. She's been on the bed thing with him, someone said she even does it on the beach. She wants to marry him. You know what girls are like, you've got two.'

'Oh yes, the penny's dropped. I saw her on the beach. They were going to have a barbecue. She swam naked and kept saying everything was super, super.' Matilda accepted an offered sherry.

' "Super" is her latest word. How one hates these expressions! At this moment in time its "super". One never had these verbal tricks oneself, one was prevented by one's parents.'

'Have you been seeing a lot of Princess Anne?'

'Why should I? We don't move in those circles, though one's not far off you know. How is Claud?'

'I thought you might ask after Louise.'

'Why? One's more interested in Claud. So like Tom isn't he – his manners, habits, you know.'

'What habits?'

'One supposes it's the genes, you know. Claud has inherited Tom's – you must have noticed – it's all genes.' Matilda listened for an unspoken 'you know' hovering at the end of the unspoken sentence. What am I doing here? Who is this dreadful woman? Where is the Anne who was once young, pretty, full of life. Who is this bore?

'Claud lives in the States. I never see him.'

'One couldn't very well go and see him, could one? One sees that.'

'Sees what?'

'One sees in Claud what you never seemed to notice in Tom. You carried it off marvellously. We all thought so, you know.'

'Are you implying Tom was a bugger?'

'Matilda!'

'Well, Claud is, "one" knows that. You seem to imply Tom was too.'

'Didn't you know?'

Matilda grinned. 'No, and nor did you. I bet you tried to get Tom into bed and he refused, so now you say he was a bugger.'

'If you weren't one of one's oldest friends –'

'How old are you, Annie?'

'Well –'

'Same age as me.'

'A good deal younger. I married when I was sixteen.'

'Anne *don't*! Not with me. Please. We are old, nearer

death than birth, time to get ready. You can't go on dyeing your hair, using silly expressions like "one" instead of "I" or "we" and mischief making.'

'I should think,' said Anne, her face clashing with her hair, 'that living as you do has softened your brain. You should come up to London oftener and keep up.'

'Keep up with what?'

'Life, of course. Life you know.'

'I am more interested in death, so should you be. You haven't much time left to be nice to poor old Humphrey. Why don't you tie up your hair and go sailing with him? Why don't you go to bed with him now and again? Have a good romp.'

'At this moment in time I don't want to.'

'Not during lunch but when he comes back from the Solent? Why not be like Vanessa? She has fun, I've seen her. Sexy.'

'You always had a vulgar streak, even at school.'

'That's like the old Anne. I'm going now. I can't take any more. I'm sorry. I don't belong any more. I'm off –'

'Leaving London?' Suddenly aware of Matilda, Anne caught her hand.

'London and life. Give my love to Humphrey.' Matilda picked up the dress in its Harrods bag.

'Don't get uptight, Matilda. You know you –'

Matilda kissed her quickly. 'I'm sorry, I must go, really sorry.'

Her lunch unfinished, Matilda got into the lift and down into the street conscious of behaving badly in her need to get away. Fool, I didn't go to the lavatory, she thought, walking quickly along the hot pavements to Piccadilly, into the Ritz where in the calm of the cloakroom she assuaged her need, washed her hands which were trembling and combed her hair. He may have slept with Lalage but he was not a bugger.

Matilda stood at a basin letting the cold tap run over her hands, wondering how to fill the afternoon until she could go back for dinner with John. The running water made her want to pee again. Sitting on the lavatory seat she remembered periods at parties when nobody had wanted to talk or dance with her and she had spent much time in cloakrooms. There had been one party which was different. She tried to remember why, in what way it had been different. Where was the party? When? What year? The memory escaped. I can't sit here the whole afternoon. This is ridiculous. She left the lavatory, washed her hands again then sat in the hall to collect herself. She felt angry that yesterday Lalage had sniped and hit and today Anne. They had attacked like birds when a member of the flock is wounded. They wanted to kill me, thought Matilda. How shocked they would be if they knew I mean to kill myself. I am already extinct, a Polish Fowl, a Tufted Hamburg. She smiled and caught the eye of an old man who was sitting near by. He winked infinitesimally. He was listening to his daughter. She must be his daughter since she addressed him as 'Papa', speaking French. Papa was to sit here and rest while she did her shopping at Fortnum's and Elizabeth Arden and Liberty's. He could rest, order tea, she would be back in an hour. Meanwhile he must rest. She went off with a cheerful wave, high heels trotting.

'Is being old very boring?' said Matilda in French.

'*Je m'emmerde, madame.*'

Matilda moved to the chair beside him.

'May I tell you what I am going to do about it for myself?'

'*Je vous en prie,*' politely.

'I am not going to get old,' said Matilda. 'I am going to kill myself.'

'You have cancer, perhaps?'

'No, no. I just refuse to suffer the horrors of age. I have had all I want. I have decided to stop.'

'How will you stop?'

Matilda outlined her picnic.

'I wish I could accompany you,' said the old man, 'but I have waited too long. I cannot walk without help, I can do nothing without help. It is undignified. Only my cat understands. I have a cat in Paris.'

Matilda told him about Gus.

'That presents a problem.'

Matilda agreed, thinking of Gus, his honking and his feet slapping on the path. She had forgotten Folly as she had forgotten Hugh.

'My daughter has gone to the shops. I must sit here and wait. I can no longer go myself. I am a prisoner of age.'

To amuse him Matilda told him about her shopping, her choice of presents for her children, of the dress she had bought that morning for the girls to quarrel over.

'That does not sound like a death wish.'

'All my cheques will bounce.'

'And you will be gone when they do?'

'That's the idea.'

'*Quelle revanche.*'

'It is my eldest son, he is such a respectable man –'

'Like his father, perhaps?'

'No, not a bit.'

'What is called "a sport"?'

'Yes, just that. Here comes your daughter. Thank you for listening to me. I should have liked to tell you about my two women friends.'

'The one who said she had slept with your husband, the other that he was homosexual?'

'How did you know?'

'That is an old trick. Have a happy death.'

'Goodbye.'

Matilda left him and, feeling cheered, took a taxi to the Hayward Gallery and thence, on her way back to John's house, to the Tate. She would have liked Claud to meet that old man. She made a quick little prayer for Claud, ejecting it from her mind like a cartoon bubble. If there was 'anybody' about to hear it, perhaps he would do something for Claud?

As she waited on the pavement outside John's house for the taxi driver to give her change she began to hum,

'There's a small hotel
By a wishing well
I wish that we were there, together.'

141

'My Mum and Dad used to sing that song.' The taxi driver counted the change into Matilda's palm. 'Said they danced to it.'

'I did too.' Matilda separated the change for the tip.

'Stood up hugging?'

'Yes, we hugged as we danced. We hung on to one another.'

'Shocking, you does that –'

'In bed?' Matilda laughed. 'We did a lot of hugging upright. I don't see the point of dancing separate from your partner.' She gave him her tip. He drove off laughing. 'Funny old girl.'

20

If Matilda had known that Hugh was spending the nights walking the countryside and swimming in the reservoir she might have worried.

He came in before dawn, slept until lunch when Mr Jones came to feed Gus, a task he had taken upon himself, and to chat. What Mr Jones wanted to chat about was Matilda.

'I love the woman.' Huw Jones sat at the kitchen table, resting his beard in his hands.

'Does she reciprocate?' Hugh was making a pot of tea.

'She does not. She was in love with Tom, that is what she thinks.'

'She wanted to die because she can no longer live without him.'

'That is the uppermost version.'

'Oh, what's underneath?'

'Who knows? Does my Matilda know herself?' Mr Jones threw out a dramatic enquiring hand. 'She has a great talent for putting matters out of her mind.'

'Your Matilda?'

'Alas not. There was an attempt, a brief scuffle it was but –'

'But what?'

'She pushed me downstairs. I might have broken a bone. I tried to clasp her in my arms but she pushed.'

'What were you doing upstairs?'

'It was the ballcock of the loo. She had asked me to mend it. I saw her great bed in her room, the bed you slept in, desecration that. I thought it would be lovely to

143

roll on the bed with Matilda so I – but she pushed and down I went. She laughed! Laughed,' he groaned.

'When was this?'

'Several years ago. Since then I keep my place.'

'But you love her?'

'Yes. Silly, isn't it?'

'Depends.'

'Of course it's silly. She is mad. She wants to die. She does not want to grow old and clutter the earth. I love her. I would look after her.'

'You would be old too.'

'Ach! We would be old together but she hates old age, refuses it. She wants to push off. It is arrogant!'

'What about her children? Can't they stop her?'

'Her children!' Mr Jones held up a finger. 'Louise, beautiful, married, two pretty tots, husband with money, lives in Paris. Louise, she is grand, she is the cat's whiskers. She has a lover, all very discreet. Then there is Mark.' Mr Jones held up a second finger. 'A right bastard, a pompous pillar of the establishment, always at conferences. I read his name in the paper. Then there is Anabel. She is flighty, a tart, hard, beautiful of course.' He lifted a third finger. 'Ah, Anabel!' A fourth finger went up. 'Claud. The youngest, a cissy, a pouf. And none of them,' Mr Jones thumped the table so that Folly barked and Gus honked, 'none of them bothers to visit their mother.'

'Perhaps she does not encourage them.'

'True, but they should try. I visit my mother in Tooting and very boring it is too.' Huw Jones laughed, tears leaping from his black eyes to flow into his beard. 'She is so boring,' he cried joyously, 'but I go. She whines, she cries, she is lonely.'

Hugh laughed with him, pouring the water into the teapot, putting the pot on the table.

'I constantly visited my mother.'

'But you murdered her.'

'I know, but she wasn't boring.'

'Tell old Jones about it.' The black eyes stopped

144

twinkling, the laughter died.

'No thanks.'

'Okay. So now we have an embarrassed pause while we think of something else to talk about.' Mr Jones was huffed.

Making toast, Hugh asked, 'And Tom, what was he really like?'

'Matilda's Tom?'

'No, yours.'

'Mine? An amusing man. Loved Matilda as well as he was able. I only knew the UFO side of him.'

'And what was that?'

'He had experience in the war, see? Brought people over from France in boats to the estuary here and in a little seaplane. So later he started smuggling, not very often, just now and then. He was a mysterious man. I think he did some work for that chap Matilda is staying with, but I'm not sure.'

'Does she know?'

'Oh no, no, no. Tom also brought in pot. He liked to smoke it just as I do. But just before he died he was cheated. Whoever sent the pot sent heroin too. Tom said he'd been double-crossed, that someone wanted to incriminate him –'

'Why did he not destroy it?'

'He did, he destroyed it, flushed it down the loo just as you did. But he told me he was keeping one packet to confront –'

'Confront who?'

'I don't know, do I? Tom went off to Paris and never came back. There have been no more little boats or little seaplanes, nothing.'

'But you go on reporting UFOs?'

'Yes I do. The police think I am harmless, so I am safe.'

'Did Matilda know of this?'

'Nothing. I think she knows nothing.'

'So she is bored.'

'Matilda is lonely, she has cranky ideas. She is middle aged, has nothing to live for so she falls in love with

145

death. There you are,' Huw Jones exclaimed. 'I am brilliant! Talking to you has discovered for me what Matilda wants. She wants death because she wants something she has never had, a splendid deduction.' Mr Jones looked enchanted.

'But we all get it. Death is the one certainty.'

'But we don't all love it, do we? It is love she wants.'

'I thought she'd had love.'

'I think,' Huw Jones said sadly, 'that she has discovered she never really had it.'

'That can't be true.'

'She could love me but she won't even try. I love her. I look after Gus when she goes away. I would die for her. I have never betrayed Tom to her. I lie at her feet and I don't get a sausage.'

Hugh gathered up the tea things, took them to the sink.

'That woman loves Gus, she does not love poor Jones.'

'Shall we play chess?' Hugh hoped that playing chess would distract his visitor. He found this talk of Matilda painful.

'Okay.' Mr Jones set up the board. 'We will play chess, stop talking about Matilda who thinks old people should not be encouraged to live, that weak babies should not be put into incubators. I think she secretly thinks it's a good thing when a lot of old people are suffocated in a fire in an old people's home, when faulty brakes fail on the buses on old people's outings, when they catch the 'flu and die by the score. She is a horrible woman, just like Hitler, and I love her and I hate her and her Death. I want to hold her in my arms and roll about in that bed.' With tears coursing down his cheeks Huw Jones set up the board. 'Your move.' His voice was desolate.

Hugh moved his Queen's pawn. I could not comfort this man, he thought, he loves his grief.

When the telephone pealed, which it did occasionally, they watched one another, counting the rings then waiting for it to stop.

'The machine is broken.'

'I taped it up for her. Stub knocked it over, he hated its noise, poor old dog.'

'She could have a new one. It looks untidy.'

Ruminating over his next move Huw Jones muttered, 'She is not a tidy woman. The house is usually a mess. She feels a mess, so death is logical, tidy.'

Thinking of his mother, Hugh exclaimed harshly, 'I don't find it tidy.'

Aware of Hugh's thought, Huw moved a threatening Bishop.

They did not hear the lorry roll to a stop in the lane, though Folly pricked her ears and Gus honked.

'Hullo,' said Claud. 'Where's Mama?'

'In London.' Hugh looked up.

'I telephoned.' Claud looked from one man to the other. 'An hour ago. I thought she must be out. She never goes away.'

'She is.' Hugh took in the full beauty of Claud in tattered jeans, worn suede jacket, Gucci shoes, dark brown eyes in sunburned face, improbable yellow hair, Matilda's mouth.

'She is away, she's staying –' began Mr Jones.

'With loverboy Sir Piers to be.'

'He's not her lover.' Mr Jones spoke crossly, jealously.

'No? Why didn't you answer the phone? Were you here?' Claud looked from one to the other. 'Oh, I *see*!' he exclaimed. 'The Matricide. Is Mama hiding you? Rather brave of her, sporting, jolly sporting. When will she be back?'

'Day after tomorrow.' Mr Jones's voice did not disguise dislike. 'Why are you here?'

'I wanted to show her my find. I've a lorry of the *most* exquisite Delabole and Serpentine headstones. She'd like them. They were in a place I heard of in Cornwall.'

'Pinched?'

'No, Jonesy, not pinched. They were being – er – moved, lined up. Car parks now not graveyards. We move with the times, move to the New World.'

'She'll be back.'

'I can't wait, have to get them packed in the container. Pity. She would have liked them. She never goes away this time of year. Sorry to miss her. Must get them shipped.'

'She –'

'She hung up on me when I phoned, cut me off. I was about to say I might be around, couldn't be sure.' He looked Hugh over, grinning slightly, Matilda's mouth, Claud's expression. 'Well then, another time. Give her my love. This her new dog? She can't live without animals.' He stroked Folly's head as she stood on her hind legs, feet braced against his thigh, tail wagging. 'Taken old Stub's place, then?' Patting the dog, he looked from one man to the other, the question 'taking my father's place?' in his eyes. 'How's her terminal illness?'

'Her *what*?'

'How's her life? Bet you've cheered her up.' He looked at Hugh. 'I shan't tell. A good lech is what she needs; a lot better for her than her infatuation with –'

'Who with?' Mr Jones's voice betrayed fear.

'Death, chap with a scythe. That one – speels it D-E-A-T-H. 'Bye then.'

They listened to his quick step, the slam of the lorry door, the engine starting up, dying away.

'Bastard! He might have told her he was coming.'

'He expected her to be here.'

'Took it for granted.'

'He did telephone. We didn't answer.'

Mr Jones was furious. 'Young sod!'

'It will be better not to tell Matilda,' Hugh said quietly, putting the chessmen away.

'Oh, much better,' Mr Jones agreed, 'much better, if better's the word.'

'Worse would be her disappointment. I've done the same –'

'Your mother wasn't like Matilda, you killed her.'

'Oh shut up about my mother you improbable fool.'

'One thinks another time will do, you are right, I do it

148

too. But my mother's so boring, so lonely, she whines at me.'

'Sod your mother.' Hugh tipped the chess board onto the floor.

21

John liked the new dress, Matilda saw at once. He seldom commented on her clothes. Walking to The Connaught from Berkeley Square where he had parked the car, she noticed too that wearing flat shoes not only allowed her to walk comfortably but made John look taller, more distinguished. Tonight he wore a dark grey flannel suit, a cream shirt and black tie. He held her arm lightly, steering her towards the restaurant.

They sat at a corner table and had a drink before ordering. Matilda told John about her day. He laughed.

'You should not take Anne and Lalage seriously.'

'But I do. They make me suffer. It is a fine art with them.'

'Rubbish.'

'They have perfected the detection of the weak point.'

'You should be safe against pinpricks.'

'I am not. I used to be better at it when Tom was alive, better in London. Now it exhausts me. I have lost my vitality.'

'I would hardly say that.' John had been amazed by her itinerary. 'You never crammed so much into two days. You would have used up two weeks in the old days.'

'Old age is creeping in.'

This irritated John, who picked up the menu. 'What will you eat?'

Sensing his irritation, Matilda obediently studied her menu, flushing slightly at his tone. Immediately John was sorry. 'You look ten years younger than our age.' There was so little between them he could safely say this.

'Our age. Yes.' Matilda flashed him a grateful smile. 'I have always envied you your assurance.'

'I always thought Tom a very lucky man.'

Matilda stifled a yawn behind the menu. Why must they talk such balls? After a lifetime knowing each other, she thought, we might have at least one absorbing topic in common. She looked at the menu and longed to be home with Gus, eating a bowl of onion soup, reading a book propped up against the teapot.

'I shall eat mussels, then salmon. I never get decent fish living so near the sea.'

'Shall you be glad to get home? Aren't you lonely?'

'No.' Matilda looked John straight in the eye. 'Not a bit.' It occurred to her that John thought she had a lover. 'I like living alone, I am used to it now. You know what it's like. Of course I'm not lonely.'

John ordered grouse. 'Why don't you change your mind and have grouse? There are no grouse in your part of the world. Oysters first.'

'All right. I gather you want to drink red wine. All right, oysters first.'

'That's about it, you read my mind.'

They ordered grouse with matchstick potatoes. John ordered a second bottle of wine. Matilda drank more than she used to, he thought, watching the way she drank, not one mouthful at a time, but two, even three, emptying the glass frequently. The wine enhanced her looks. He told her about a very beautiful villa where he had stayed that spring.

'In France?'

'No, Italy. Marvellous wild flowers in April, one can still find so many different kinds of orchids.'

'I'd rather you didn't come to my funeral, John, Piers I mean.'

'What?'

'I said I'd rather you didn't come to my funeral.'

'I was telling you about Italy. Weren't you listening?'

'Only half. I'm obsessed by death.'

151

'All right, we'll talk about it. Why don't you want me to come?'

'You get too close. You think I have a lover.'

'It occurred to me.'

'Mr Jones made an advance.'

'That fellow with a beard, that fat bald chap? What cheek.'

'No it wasn't. He isn't fat, he is square. He can't help being bald. It was very sweet of him really.'

'Sweet!'

'You talk as though –' Matilda stopped, realizing the unwisdom of what she was about to say. I do not belong to John, she thought. He mustn't get that idea in his head. She drank more wine.

'I'm verging on tipsy.' But John was looking towards the entrance. Matilda followed his glance.

'Oh Christ!'

Strolling in, cool, young, exquisite, came Anabel, followed by a very tall black man with quite extraordinarily beautiful features. Anabel was laughing up at him, her teeth, larger than Matilda's, flashing, her face alight with the joy of conquest.

'What a wonderful young man. Who is he?' Matilda had jerked into sobriety.

'Quite a sizeable fish at the U.N.'

'Is his wife beautiful?'

'Yes, a very brilliant woman.'

'Poor Anabel.'

But Anabel had seen them. She came forward in a rush.

'Ma! How super to see you! No wonder I couldn't get you on the phone, you were up here with your beau all the time. How are you, Piers darling? This is Aron, Ma, isn't he exquisite?' Matilda shook a firm hand. 'Oh, Ma, what a dress! You do look wonderful, doesn't she look wonderful?' Her great eyes swivelled from John to her escort. 'Wonderful!'

'Won't you join us?'

'Oh, no, darling, we can't. We only came in for a drink.

How is home? How is Stub? How is Prissy?'

'They have both been dead for a long time.' Matilda felt no anger.

'And Gus?'

'He's alive.'

'He'll be next then, won't he?' Anabel let out the words with a yelp of laughter.

When Anabel and her man had gone Matilda began to laugh. 'It's the surprise! The surprise I have every time I meet her that I in my belly created that girl.'

John grinned.

'How long has she been in London? You always know everything.'

'About three months.'

'Little bitch. Couldn't get me on the phone. I suppose the others have been over too?'

'Not Claud, I haven't seen him.'

'His teeth are better than Anabel's and he doesn't go about with his mouth open. He telephoned me, you needn't cover for him.'

'Don't be a cat, Matty. Anabel probably has adenoids. You're her mother, you should have seen to them. How long is he here for?'

'Girls with protruding teeth always get men, it makes them look amiable. Oh, Claud – he went to Yorkshire.'

'Have another drink.'

'I see why people become alcoholics. They learn to accept. No thank you, no more.'

'You must learn to accept your children.'

'Why should I?' Matilda was suddenly extremely angry. 'Why? I don't like any of them except Claud. Let them come to my funeral. I don't want you but I do want them. How dare she not know about Stub and Prissy?'

'Perhaps you didn't tell her.'

'I'm sure I didn't.'

'Well then.'

'Well nothing. I want to go home.'

'We will.' John waved to the waiter. 'I'll take you home.'

'Not yours, mine. I must get back. It's nothing but stab, stab, stab in London.' In an unconscious gesture Matilda cupped her breasts in her hands, then folded them in front of her on the table.

'D'you know that someone somewhere put his hands over my breasts and said, "Chimborazo Catapaxi has stolen my heart –" '

'I should think lots of chaps did.' John was signing the bill and counting money for the tip. 'That was one of the poems our generation quoted like *A Shropshire Lad* and one or two particular sonnets we'd done at school.'

'How bracing you are.' Matilda stood up. John followed her out thinking that after all that wine she was wonderfully steady on her pins.

Arriving back in Chelsea, Matilda's mood changed. She hummed and sang snatches of Cole Porter. John joined in.

'A lovely evening, so educational.' She watched him lock the car, standing in her flat shoes on the pavement, still warm from the long hot summer. John opened the door and they went in.

'A nightcap?'

'An Alka-Seltzer more like.'

'I'll get you one.'

Matilda kicked off her shoes and spread her toes.

'You and your feet.' John stood in the doorway, holding the Alka-Seltzer, smiling indulgently.

'My country feet.' She pulled at the toes of her tights, easing the constriction.

'Have you seen my bedroom?'

'No.'

'You are wonderfully incurious, Matty. Come and look.' Matilda followed him across the landing.

'New curtains.'

'Very pretty. Where did you get that stuff?'

'Paris.'

'They are not like you somehow –' She was puzzled. 'More Tom's sort of thing.'

'He got it for me.'

154

Just one more prick in the heart, thought Matilda, keeping her face blank. Trust John.

Pulling the pink dress over her head she was dazzled by the momentary darkness. Whoops! I'm tipsy! Carefully she put the dress on a hanger, turning it this way and that to see whether she had spilled food on it. She took off her knickers and bra. Her head was singing, it was difficult to focus. In the bathroom she mixed Alka-Seltzer and drank the noxious mixture, sitting naked on the edge of the bath, expecting to throw up.

After a few minutes she put on her nightdress and got into bed. She kept the bedside light on. If she turned it off her head would whirl.

She said a little prayer asking for sleep.

No sleep.

She lay thinking about Anabel. So beautiful. A horrid girl on the whole. She had never been able to communicate with her, nor with Louise or Mark, only Claud, and even then only on occasion. It is my fault, she reproached herself. I cannot reach them any more than my mother could reach me. I am not wanted. What could I have said to Anabel? Something warm, loving, maternal. I felt none of those things. I felt resentful. She never comes near me. I should have made friends with that man, he would then be kinder to Anabel, dispose of her less lightly. I don't mind her going about with a black man. Why should I? Stub was black.

That's it. Matilda drunkenly saw her nature revealed. I can only get on with animals. I only trust animals. Stub, Prissy, Gus, all the animals in her past, as demanding as children but never nasty. Wow! Black, brown, multi-coloured animals. Ah! She loved them.

Gosh, she thought, I'm never going to sleep. She put on her dressing-gown, put out the light, opened the window and leant out. Somewhere in London lovely Anabel lay in that man's arms. I envy her. I hope he will not hurt her. It will make her take it out on someone else, some white dolt. Anabel, so self-assured, no great animal lover she. Matilda remembered Anabel drowning a rabbit in a bucket. Bloody child. In a way she was like Tom. This unforeseen thought caused Matilda to weep. She walked up and down the room weeping. 'Tom, Tom, oh poor Tom, did I love you?'

Matilda felt so uncertain she became distraught. I must walk, she thought, putting on her slippers. She wrapped the dressing-gown round her, took her latchkey, tiptoed downstairs, letting herself out into the street.

Roused by the slight sound, John looked out onto the landing, wondering what the hell Matilda was doing now.

'What on earth is going on? he called querulously.

'I'm going for a fucking walk.' Matilda slammed the street door.

'If anyone behaved like that to me.' Matilda said aloud in the empty street, 'I'd never have them in my house again.' She walked weeping along the pavements, composing nice things she should have said to Anabel, clever intelligent things she could have said to the beautiful black man. Aron – a splendid name – balanced, biblical, dignified. My word, she thought, he was sexy, no wonder Anabel – do hope she enjoys it, lucky girl.

She walked briskly, passing the Royal Hospital, far from John's house. The Alka-Seltzer was working. She turned left through Burton Court, into Smith Street, along the King's Road. A middle-aged widow, she saw herself walking down the King's Road in her dressing-gown, sober now. It was a pity that she liked animals best, but there it was. At some moment, she could not remember when, she had nearly loved human beings. It must have been a moment of passion. Passion was something so tremendously rare. Animals were better, safer, Now she was nearly back at the cul-de-sac. The latchkey? She had it in her hand. I couldn't bear to wake him again, she thought, letting herself in quietly. He may have owned Tom but he doesn't own me. She shut the door and crept up to bed.

22

In the train Matilda leafed through *Harper's*, a luxury
bought for her by John with *The Times* and the *Guardian*.
He had found her a seat. kissed her goodbye and left
before the train started, putting her out of his mind
before he reached his car.

Matilda, too, had forgotten John, it dawning on her
that for four days in London she had not listened to the
news or read a paper. This had happened to her before.
Usually she found she had missed nothing and what
news there was was fresh and interesting.

She had hardly thought of Hugh since visiting his flat.
Now, skipping through the *Guardian*, it seemed silly to
have bothered to snatch him a pair of shoes. Any man in
his senses would have long since left and be far away.
He had no real need of the money. A man ingenious
enough to keep a cache under the communal carpet of a
house full of flats would be clever enough to have moved
on. The probability was there and as the train moved out
into open country she hoped it was a certainty.

Matilda laid *Harper's* down. Its contents were a catalogue of the shops she had visited. The train, gathering
speed, rocked along by the Kennet and Avon canal.
Harrods, Fortnum's, Habitat and Liberty's seemed to
her more like museums than places where persons like
herself shopped. She was glad she had sent her children
presents and that from a flower shop in Knightsbridge
she had arranged for an exotic fern to be delivered to
John with a note of thanks. She would write an apology
too. A group of geese crossing a farmyard seen from the

train made her feel intensely anxious. If Hugh had left would Gus be starving when she got back? Normally if she went away she would ask Mr Jones to keep an eye on Gus, but Hugh did not know Mr Jones and would have left Gus to his own devices. Nervously, as though the action would make the train go faster, she felt in her bag for the keys of her car. For the rest of the journey she held them in her hand.

Anxiety bunched her stomach. She shook her head when the attendant came down the corridor calling 'First Lunch,' then 'Second Lunch,' then 'Coffee, Tea, Ices.' All she could think of was Gus starving. She had shown Hugh the maize bin. Perhaps he would have gone off leaving a large basin of maize and a bucket of water. If he had let Gus out to fend for himself the neighbourhood fox would have killed him.

Then again perhaps Hugh was still there. He had food for some days. All he was short of was milk. She had made him promise to be careful, to keep quiet, to keep hidden. She wondered how she had got herself into this situation, it was lunatic. Obviously, she thought, clutching the car keys, by now something would have happened to alert the police. The dog would have barked, Hugh would have been seen, arrested after a chase, be 'helping the police with their enquiries'. Why had she not read the papers or listened to the news?

Of course John was joking when he said he was meeting the Matricide in Prague. He read the papers, would have taken it for granted she did too, would have made his joke. Oh God, thought Matilda, he must think I'm mad. Perhaps I am. It's high time I replanned my picnic or I shall end my days in a bin. Too boring for Louise, Mark, Anabel and Claud. I care for them enough not to inflict that on them. The car keys bit into her palm.

She made an effort towards calm and how to react to the police when they told her they had found Hugh. It would be best to be flustered, astonished, indignant. Then, remembering Hugh's shoes were in her suitcase, she thought, how incriminating, I must throw them out of the window, and stood up to reach for her case on the rack, when she noticed the train slowing down. She had reached her destination.

23

The car was where she had left it, exactly the same, just a bit more dusty. Somebody had written in the dirt on the back windows:

The driver of this car is a sex maniac.

Matilda put the key in the lock. The car was airless. She opened the windows, starting the engine, letting it idle. The palm of her hand felt sore from clutching the keys. As the engine livened she thought she would never know whether those hints dropped about Tom were true. As she drove out of the station yard she told herself she didn't care whether he had been a part-time spy, slept around or been a bugger. It made no difference now.

Driving through the town she saw faces light up with laughter as people read the message on the back window. It's great to look respectable, she thought. Then she thought it must even soften the hearts of the police who would be waiting for her. If Hugh has any gratitude he will have broken a window to make it look like a break-in, messed things up a bit, not too much, just enough.

She stopped to buy milk, then drove fast along the road bordered by bristly cornfields waiting for the plough, pheasants gleaming in the stubble. She felt hot and sticky after the train, looked forward to changing into old clothes. It felt warm enough to swim, make a trip to the sea. As soon as she had dealt with the police she would go.

In the three miles of lanes from the main road to her cottage, late holidaymakers were sticking firmly to the middle of the road, determined not to scratch their paint against the tall banks of this alien countryside. Their care was alarming to Matilda, used to judging the width by a whisker.

She opened the gate, drove into the garage. She switched off the engine. Silence, then a loud honk and the slap of Gus's feet as he came to meet her.

'So you are all right my handsome, my gorgeous brute.' Gus flapped his wings, excreted.

'All alone?' She stroked his neck. Gus honked louder, walked slightly ahead towards the back door. Matilda listened. Not a soul about, no Panda car, no surprises. She felt a sense of loss. Hugh had gone just as she had thought he would, as she had hoped he would.

My Christ, Matilda said to herself, what a fake I am. I am sadly disappointed. What shall I do with his shoes and his money? He might have waited, might have trusted me.

Crossly she felt for the key under the scraper and opened the door. The house was orderly and empty, as empty as when she had closed the door and set off for her picnic.

'Damn, blast and to hell with that barbecue,' she said to Gus, who craned his neck in at the door, blue eyes meeting hers. 'That bloody girl Vanessa and her Bobby.'

'I wasn't expecting you back so soon.' Hugh, followed by Folly, walked in past Gus. 'Hullo there.' He bent and kissed her cheek. Matilda burst into tears.

'What's up?' Hugh stood back while Folly leapt up, wagging her tail in ecstasy, scratching Matilda's London clothes. 'What are the tears for?'

'I was expecting the police to be waiting for me. I was all ready.'

'All keyed up?'

'Yes.'

'No police, sorry. Were you hoping?'

'I thought you'd gone.'

'Sorry, I haven't.'

'I brought your money and a pair of shoes.'

'Oh good, I need shoes. Well done.'

161

'But I absolutely felt you'd be gone or that they would have caught you. I saw it all in my mind.'

'So you're disappointed.'

'God, no, I'm –' Matilda pretended to herself she did not know what she was feeling.

'Don't tell me you're pleased.'

'Very,' Matilda whispered. 'Very pleased.'

'Ah,' Hugh took her face in his hands and gently kissed her mouth. 'Nice to see you back, sex maniac.'

Matilda giggled. 'Some naughty child.'

'Did you have a good time?' Hugh was filling the kettle, putting out cups while Matilda, in her London clothes, watched him.

'Not really. No. I had good meals, went round the shops, saw people –'

'Friends?'

'They used to be friends.'

'Not any more?'

'One suggested Tom was a bugger, another that she'd slept with him and the friend I was staying with had the nerve to hint that Tom was a spy.'

Hugh laughed. 'Strong or weak? India or China?' He held a tea-spoon in one hand, a caddy in the other.

'Strong Indian.'

Hugh made the tea.

'It's been pretty boring here without you. If it hadn't been for Mr Jones I might have left.'

'Have you met him? Oh my!'

'Yes. Day after you left. He came to tell you he'd seen a UFO. He and I play chess.'

Matilda kicked off her shoes, sat at the kitchen table. 'He used to play with Tom.'

'So he says.'

'Has he told anybody you are here? Who does he think you are?'

'He says he never sees anybody except you as they think he is barmy. I like him. He plays a very odd game.'

'Tom said he cheated.'

Matilda took from her bag the envelopes, handing them to Hugh. 'What made you think of hiding it in such a public place?'

'My brother and I used to dream up places, have competitions between ourselves when we were children.'

'The Major with the nose?'

'Yes. Life was simpler then. We trusted each other. It was like Mr Jones. He trusts me. I trust him.'

'When did he see the UFO?'

'Day you left. He's coming presently for a game and supper.'

'It's not safe.'

'I can't tell him not to come. It would upset him.'

'A secret between two people is a secret, but not between three. More than three, I daresay. He's really crazy.'

'No, no,' said Hugh comfortably. 'He is eccentric. He likes to talk, he's lonely.'

Matilda groaned, put down her cup and went up to have a bath, running the water very deep, almost hotter than she could bear, to wash away insinuations about Tom. She came down to find Hugh and Mr Jones lying on the grass, chatting in the dark.

'Mr Jones, Huw, how nice.'

Mr Jones scrambled to his feet, short, square with his beard grey on the chin, brown at the sides, his black eyes observant and bright.

'I brought a bottle with me.' Mr Jones held Matilda's hand between both of his, squeezing it reassuringly before letting it go.

'Oh, how kind.' She tried to enthuse.

'Not dandelion, whisky.' Mr Jones smiled shyly. 'From the pub.'

'I'll fetch some glasses.' Hugh went into the house.

'How was London?' Mr Jones asked politely.

'So, so.'

'Nice to get home then?'

'Yes.'

'I was delighted to find Hugh here when I came to see

163

you. I would have been disappointed to find the house empty.'

Hugh came out carrying a tray with water and glasses. Mr Jones ignored him. 'It is important to help Hugh.'

'Help? In what way?'

'Oh, give him a lift.' Mr Jones reached out to take a glass from Hugh and passed it to Matilda. 'I am interested in the extreme.'

'What do you mean?'

Mr Jones took the glass Hugh offered. 'Just a little water. It's extreme to kill your mother.' He sipped his drink, eyes downcast.

Matilda couldn't see Hugh's face. She let out her breath. 'You sly old boots.'

Mr Jones swallowed a gulp of whisky. 'I am neither sly nor mad. I listen to the radio and read the papers. I mind my own business. You should know that, Matilda. Hugh knows it.'

'After all these years I certainly should.'

Mr Jones looked gravely at Hugh then at Matilda. 'It seemed to me no business of mine to inform on your visitor and Tom never informed on me so fair dos, I thought, finding Hugh Warner here, fair dos.'

'We, I mean I, never believed –' Matilda hesitated.

'Never believed in the UFOs?'

'Well, not really.'

'Just as well, nobody else does, so in return I do not believe in the Matricide. You *cannot*,' Mr Jones leaned forward to put a hand on Matilda's knee, 'you cannot believe all you read in the papers or hear on the radio, that's a fact.'

'It is.'

'Mind you,' Mr Jones laughed, 'I don't suppose he ever told you.'

'He didn't. I only found out after his death.'

'Well then, you know now. Sorry.'

'For the last few days almost everyone I've met has been hinting at a Tom I didn't know. I thought that was

164

spiteful London but now you do it too.' Matilda paused. 'He hid things from me.'

'Not telling is not necessarily hiding. He knew and I knew if he upset me about the UFOs I'd take umbrage. I would have stopped him, so he said nothing, that's all'. Mr Jones finished his whisky, put his glass down on the grass and sprang to his feet without using his hands.

'We'll play chess another day,' he said to Hugh, shook Matilda's hand and walked off jauntily.

'Well!' Matilda sat back on the grass, stretching her legs, 'I'm blowed! What a simpleton I've been. It never dawned on me he and Tom were partners.'

'You look shocked.' Hugh gathered Folly into his arms. 'You must have had an inkling.'

'None. It was after Tom's death I found –' She hesitated.

'Evidence.' Hugh was smiling, his teeth foxy. 'Pot and heroin.'

'You've been prying.'

'Surely you didn't expect me not to?'

'Rather ungentlemanly.' Matilda's voice was tart. Then she giggled. 'What did you find?'

'Heroin. I flushed it away. What did you do with the pot?'

'Smoked it.'

'All of it?'

'No.'

'Where is it?'

'In the bank.'

'And you say under a stair carpet is imaginative.'

'I didn't have much left. I packed it into a silver cigarette box of my grandfather's and left it for Claud. He likes it.'

'How much did you use?'

'Don't know. It lasted some months after Tom –' She sat up suddenly. 'D'you think Tom really had his heart attack in the rue Jacob or d'you think it was in Louise's bed? She lives just round the corner, she could have pushed him out.'

'Don't be vile,' Hugh shouted at her. 'Don't imagine worse than you need. He was probably on his way to see her.' He was very angry.

'Yes, I expect you are right. One thinks such dreadful thoughts. That's why I smoked pot. The hallucinations are mostly nice.'

Hugh refilled her glass, put it in her hand. 'Tell me about Louise.'

Matilda did not look at him. She sat, the glass in one hand and with the other hand stroking Gus, who had come to stand beside her.

'She was our first child, a love child. Tom was crazy about her. I was pregnant when we married. I don't like babies much. I prefer animals.' Gus sank down beside her, his neck twisted, blue eye looking up at her. 'Tom looked after the baby better than I did. He changed her nappies, washed her, fed her, had her in bed when she cried, cuddled her, was marvellous really. She adored him. It was always Tom she loved, not me. I suppose in the event they were so close nappy changing evolved into fucking. I should not have been surprised.'

Hugh said nothing, watching her face, as did the gander.

'I loved Tom,' she said quietly. 'They didn't see me when I found them in my bed, well, our bed I suppose. I went for a walk and had a think. I couldn't stop loving Tom. I loved Louise, not as much as Claud but I did love her, so I decided half Tom was better than no Tom. I never told him I knew.'

'Go on.'

'I thought when Louise married it would stop.'

'Did it?'

'No it did not.' She flushed. 'It became more so. Tom brought home lots of new bedtime tricks. I pretended I didn't notice.' She glanced at Hugh. 'I enjoyed them. I felt a bit funny learning new aspects of sex from my daughter but it's true, I liked it.' She grinned at Hugh. 'I tell you everything, don't I?'

Hugh felt he had had enough of Louise, that it was

166

better to leave Louise while she was tasting good. 'Tell me about Jones. Have you slept with him?'

'Does he say I have?'

'No, but I wasn't sure.'

'I haven't. He wanted to and there was a time when I might have. He is such a contrast to Tom, all that hair and short legs, but Anabel – oh!' Matilda gave a shriek of laughter which she tried to stifle, putting her hand across her mouth.

'Anabel?' Hugh probed.

Tears of laughter oozing from the corners of her eyes, Matilda gasped. 'It's so unkind to laugh. Anabel had come. It was after Tom had been dead some time, a year perhaps. Mr Jones was being helpful, so kind, weeding the garden. I'd let it go dreadfully. Anabel was with me in the kitchen. She'd just said in an arrogant, bossy voice, "Ma, you should brace up. What you need is sex. It's very bad to stop suddenly and give it up altogether. You've tried pot," she said – I don't know how she knew – "you've tried pot and it doesn't do anything for you, you must have sex. Why not," said Anabel, fixing me with those great brown eyes, "have old Jones? Do him a favour. You know he pines for you." ' Matilda wiped the tears with her finger. 'We looked at him. He was crouching there wearing wide khaki shorts and his balls were hanging down over the carrot leaves. Oh!' Matilda's eyes filled again. 'I've never been so close to that girl. She said, "They look like nutbags you hang out for the tits. Sorry I spoke." Poor girl. She laughed until she threw up and Mr Jones came in and made us a resuscitating cuppa. He thought we were crying over Tom. That was the last time she came here. I saw her in London. She came into the Connaught looking lovely with the most beautiful man. John, Sir Piers to be, knew him. She wasn't expecting to see me. She carried it off rather well.'

'You didn't know she was in London?'

'No. She had not wanted to see me. I might have asked her to visit me. It's a risk.' Matilda shook her head. 'Poor

Mr Jones.' Hugh felt it safer to leave Anabel sick with laughter.

'So Mr Jones's UFOs?'

'Why are you changing the subject?'

'That's the art of conversation – edge. Did you know about the UFOs, what they were?'

'Not until I found the drugs after Tom's death. While he was alive it all went on under my nose so . . .' She seemed unwilling even now to say more.

'So?' Hugh pressed.

'So if he was a smuggler and I didn't know, it may well be true that he slept with Lalage as well as Louise and that he was one of the next-honours-list Sir Piers's spies. But I cannot see him as a bugger, as Anne suggests.'

'Would you have loved him less?'

'No. I loved him. If you need proof there's Louise. No divorce.'

'You couldn't cite your own daughter.'

'I don't see why not. I thought of doing it but it wouldn't have altered anything. Louise is married to a man I like, it would have broken him, whereas you –'

'Whereas I, who have killed my mother, can understand, is that it?'

'I suppose so.'

'Tom and Louise didn't kill anything or anybody.'

'How d'you know?'

'What are you suggesting now?'

'Louise's second child is abnormally like Tom.'

'You repellent woman! It's well known children take after their grandparents. Louise would never have let herself –'

'Conceive her father's child?'

'That's what I mean.'

'You don't know Louise.'

'She sounds very like you.' Hugh's voice expressed disgust.

'She's very like me, very like indeed. Tom always said so.' Matilda laughed. Hugh joined in the infection.

'The Egyptians, the Pharoahs.' Matilda grinned at

168

Hugh. 'If they did it, why not Tom and Louise?'

Hugh left the question unanswered, setting himself to opening the envelopes and counting the money.

'How much?' Matilda watched him.

'Quite a lot. Enough to get away. When my brother gets back, if he ever does, he will find the cache gone. He'll know.'

'But he won't tell.'

'Money is funny stuff, it does things to people. If he is needing a couple of thousand and it's gone, he may well be irked. So –'

'So you'd better go.'

'Yes,'

'How?'

'Like everyone else – train and plane on a busy day. Passport Control are very pushed, all those faces just become a blur.'

'Why not a boat? One of the UFOs?'

'That has stopped. I wouldn't involve him anyway. I like him.'

'What about me? I'm involved.'

'Like you say, you're a dead woman.'

'And you don't like me. Repellent, you said. Evil.'

'Truthful. Truth may be a laughing matter but it is quite refreshing. Shall you miss me?'

'I shall plan my picnic.' She would not answer directly. 'You can stay as long as you like,' she added quickly.

'What about Gus.'

'I love him.'

'That's true, an uncomplex love to you, easy, but the poor bird's so twisted he kills a goose when put with one.'

Matilda wasn't listening to him. She tapped her teeth with her empty glass.

'John, Sir Piers to be, was in this somewhere. I believe he was in on the smuggling thing. I think he and Tom worked together or Tom worked for him. I had the impression in London that he was trying to find out if I

169

knew. No, that's not right; I have the impression now. He said he was meeting you in Prague.'

'What did you say?'

'I pretended to believe him, played along. I didn't exactly want to tell him you were here. He's sinister.'

'Maybe my brother is one of his minions infiltrating the Guerillas or some ploy of that kind. They train in Prague.'

Matilda stood up suddenly, startling Folly. 'All I really mind,' she said bitterly, 'is being left out. I feel such a fool left out of the *fun*.'

'Hurt pride.'

'Of course my pride's hurt, battered.'

Hugh said nothing, finding no word of comfort.

Matilda lay in bed that night hugging the bedclothes, full of suspicions. The annihilation of her pride was complete.

24

Equally perturbed, for he had no reason to hurt her, Hugh woke Mr Jones in his bungalow, inviting himself in for a drink. Pleased to be needed, the lonely man arose, wrapped an old kimono round his hairy person, took the whisky from its cupboard, found glasses and set up the chessboard.

'Your mind is not on the game,' he presently said, checkmating Hugh too easily.

'I have hurt Matilda.'

'She is vulnerable.'

'How did her husband manage?'

'He had the knack. She is not all that bright.'

'Bright?'

'That is what I said. She is young for her age, she believes what she wishes to, always deludes herself.'

'I think she is getting over it.'

'A pity for her.'

'Why?'

'Well,' Mr Jones looked uneasy, 'it is far better for her to remember Tom as she liked to have him.'

'You are ambiguous.'

'Tom had her caged where he wanted her. She never knew he was a rogue, dishonest you might say, but there you are, she loved him.'

'She loves that goose.'

'It's the same thing. Her gander is a fantasy, so was her husband, but she was satisfied, thought they'd live and die together. It was tommy rot, romantic. Tom would not have killed himself before he got old to save people

171

trouble. My God, he would not. No, no, he would have had Louise, Mark, Anabel and Claud belting round waiting on him in his invalid chair.'

'And Matilda?'

'He would have let her die first, worked her to death and made her enjoy it.'

'It sounds just as well for Matilda he died in Paris.'

'I don't think so.' Mr Jones yawned and scratched his hairy chest. 'She is finding out more about him, liking him less, getting disillusioned, it is a pity.'

'She will find a modus vivendi.'

'Not Matilda. Whatever anyone does she will remain what she is. She and the gander are well suited.'

'I think she will kill herself. She should have some fun first though, take a lover, go abroad –'

'She has no wish to go abroad. She has the goose.'

'Gander.'

'Okay. Now what did you wake me up for in truth?' Hugh laughed.

'Can you, if I give you the money, get me some foreign currency?'

'Sure, of course I can.' Mr Jones did not add that he had a trunkful of German marks and Swiss francs as he did not think Hugh would believe him. 'How much have you got?'

'A thousand.'

'Bring it to me tomorrow. Do you want to go over in the UFO? Nice boat. It's in the harbour.'

'No. I shall go from London Airport, it's the most crowded.'

'Very good, you do that. That is how your murdered mother would travel.'

Hugh answered shortly, 'There is no need to harp.'

'Takes all sorts. Louise, Mark, Anabel and Claud would not kill their mother, only want to.'

'Poor Matilda.'

'She has the goose.' Mr Jones had begun to look sleepy. Hugh got up.

'I will bring the money tomorrow in cash.'

172

'I will have the currency ready for you in a few days.'

I bet he has it stashed around the bungalow thought Hugh. He said goodnight and walked back to the cottage.

Gus, recognizing his step, gave a token honk from the scullery. As he climbed the stairs Hugh heard Matilda's snores. By morning, he thought, she will have forgotten her unease, have buried the discoveries about Tom in her unconscious.

He stood in the dark, looking out of his window at the moonlit countryside, thinking of his mother, remembering her face looking up at him in terror and hearing her voice – 'Oh Hugh, quick, *please*.' Her eyes large, stone grey, fringed with, for an old woman, ridiculously long lashes, haunted him. He recollected how, as a boy at school, homesick, unable to sleep, he had tried to bring her face and voice to mind for comfort in the alien environment of his dormitory. He had had trouble in those days to see her clearly; now he both saw her and heard her voice. 'Oh Hugh, quick, *please*.' She would travel with him whether he willed it or not.

Hugh made his arrangements without consulting Matilda. While she was shopping he tried on Tom's clothes, looking at himself in the glass, wearing various garments. Tom's taste in dress was unlike his own. He felt unnatural in most of the clothes. From a store of trousers, jeans, suits, shirts, jerseys, he made a final choice of pale corduroy trousers, a tweed jacket, red socks. He hesitated whether to wear a polo neck jersey or a shirt, settling for the shirt as more respectable. He put aside, for packing, jeans, T-shirts, spare pants, a shirt or two, swimming trunks and sweaters. Ranging round the house he found several pairs of black glasses.

He dressed himself and waited for Matilda, listening for her car, standing out of sight in the hall. When the car drew up Gus honked from the back door and slapped his feet as he ran to meet her. Listening to her voice greeting the bird Hugh thought she sounded younger, happier, altogether more cheerful and full of confidence.

She dumped her parcels on the kitchen table. 'Wait, Gus, wait,' she said to the bird. 'I'll get you some maize.' She kicked off her espadrilles. Her feet were barely audible on the stone floor. 'Here,' she said, 'here, Gus, my love, eat this.' She put the bowl on the step and straightened up. Catching sight of Hugh in the doorway she gasped.

'Hullo,' she said, 'were you looking for me?' Hugh came forward a step. 'Or my husband?' Matilda's voice tightened. 'He's around somewhere, I'll call him.' She raised her voice and called loudly, 'Tom. Darling? There's a man here to see you –' She edged towards the telephone.

'Matilda.' Hugh stepped forward. 'It's me, don't be frightened.'

'Oh!' Matilda whispered. 'My God, you scared me. I nearly wet my knickers. How d'you do it? You've changed yourself completely. I thought you were the police.' She sat down abruptly.

'It's good, isn't it?' Hugh turned around so that she could see him. 'What do you think?'

'Those trousers were Mark's.'

'Not Tom's?'

'No, and the jacket was Claud's until he took to wearing suede. Where did you find the glasses?'

'In the hall cupboard.'

'Those were Anabel's when enormous lenses were in fashion. They make your nose quite small. What's this in aid of?'

'I want to get out. I'm getting claustrophobia. I feel like taking you out to lunch and a swim. What do you say?'

'Risky.'

'I have to start some time. Come on, it will give me confidence if I'm with you.'

'We can't start off together, nobody knows you are here.'

'Very well. I'll go through the copse and meet you at the bus stop.'

'I must change my clothes, get my bathing things. I don't think you should risk it.'

'Come on, Matilda, try.'

'Wait a minute then.'

Matilda went upstairs and snatched up a cardigan, put on a clean shirt, combed her hair, excited.

'Okay, I'm ready.'

'Give me ten minutes' start.' Hugh left the house.

Ten minutes gives me time to ring the police. Ten minutes gives me time to make a plan with them. She watched the clock jerk its minute hand. 'Ten minutes is a life,' she said to Gus as she filled his bowl with maize. 'Why does he tempt me with ten minutes?' She locked the back door, put the key under the scraper, went to the car and sat with her eyes on her watch until the ten minutes had passed.

Hugh sat on a stile by the bus stop, Folly beside him. He got in beside Matilda. Folly sat behind.

'First mistake was to bring Folly. She's been seen with me. People think she's mine. You mustn't do that again.'

'Right, I won't.'

'You shouldn't have given me ten minutes. I might have phoned the police.'

'But you didn't?'

'No, but please don't do it again. I thought of doing it.'

Hugh laughed. 'There are two Matildas, one who phones the police and one who is kind and loves Gus. For all I know there are many more; those are just the two I've met.'

'How many of you?'

'Count.'

'There's you hunted, about to go out with the tide. There's you with Folly. There's you with Gus. There's you with me. There's you –'

'Killing my mother.'

'I wasn't going to say that.'

'You were. Be honest, stay honest. We are near death, both of us.'

'All right, there's you killing your mother. End of conversation.'

Angrily, Matilda trod on the accelerator and drove fast on the main road.

'Don't drive so fast, there's a Panda car behind you.'

Matilda slowed, letting the police car overtake them. 'I'm frightened every time I see them. I was brought up to like them.'

'So was I.' Hugh looked at her profile. 'Where's the best place to eat?'

'We'd better go somewhere quiet.'

'No, I want a busy place. I don't want a quiet place, as though I were hiding.'

'All right. The best place is the Crab Inn if we can get a table.'

'Does it have a bar?'

'Yes.'

'Right. Take us there.'

Matilda parked the car. They made their way to the restaurant along the crowded street. Hugh held Matilda's arm, liking the feel of her skin, glancing about him at the people.

The Crab Inn was crowded. They agreed to wait for a table.

'Let's sit outside. Can we eat out, it's pleasant.'

They were told they could. Hugh ordered drinks, sat facing Matilda who, with the sun in her eyes, screwed up her nose and sneezed.

'I forgot my dark glasses.'

'Stay here. I'll get you some. Sit in my place.' He did not offer Anabel's glasses.

'I'll come too.'

'Wait here. If there's a free table, take it, start ordering. I shan't be long.' Hugh loped off up the street. He bought a plain pair of dark glasses for Matilda, guessing at the fit, then went to a travel agency. He enquired the times of trains to London before strolling back to Matilda.

'They are just getting us a table overlooking the harbour.'

'Nice.' He handed her the dark glasses.

'Thank you.' She put them on.

A waiter brought the menu. Hugh asked for the wine list.

'What's good here?'

'They do a delicious smoked trout paté. The crab's always good. Sometimes they do a lovely goat cheese with garlic, blows your head off.'

'We could finish with that. I shall have the trout paté. What's the steak like today, waiter?'

'Well – sir –'

'Okay, not steak then. I'll have the gigot of lamb, the paté first and the goat's cheese. What will you have Matilda?'

'Just the gigot, the cheese and salad.'

'And a bottle of No. 17 please.' The waiter scribbled on his pad.

'It's a nice place and Folly can sit with us.' Hugh smiled across at Matilda who looked at him anxiously. She made a tiny sideways gesture with her thumb. Behind his dark glasses Hugh let his eyes swivel without moving his head. A rather vacuous girl sat at a table with her parents who were stolidly eating their pudding. The girl had finished eating and was idly flipping through the *Express*.

'It says the police have a line on the Matricide, Mummy, and they are charging the dog-eater.'

'The what, dear?'

'The Matricide, Mummy, he's been seen in Paris on a barge on the Seine.'

'Can't think why they haven't caught the fellow.'

'Oh, Daddy, he's clever, grown a beard, it says here, a red beard.'

'Have they arrested him, dear?'

'No, Mummy, it says here one of his best friends recognized him.'

'Can't be his best friend if he tells the police.'

'Oh, Daddy, he'd have to! He did murder his mother after all.'

'Bribed I expect.'

'Who's bribed?'

'Someone's bribed the police. What the hell do I pay my taxes for, I'd like to know, if they can't catch a simple murderer. Waiter, my bill.'

'I don't think he's so simple.'

'Don't contradict your father, dear.'

'I wish you wouldn't call me "dear", Mummy, My name is Inez.'

'I know, dear, we chose it for you.'

'There you go again, *dear*! It's common to say "dear"

178

all the time. Why can't you call me Inez or "darling". "Darling" is all right.'

'So you call your mother common do you? You'll be murdering her next.'

'Oh Daddy, I'd never.'

'Call me Dad. Dad's common. This is a bloody expensive lunch.'

'Poor man, I expect he regrets it now. Such a large nose. Rather an attractive man from the photograph.'

'Mummy! Your taste, really!'

'Well, dear, you can be both, dear, attractive and a murderer. D'you want to powder your nose before we go to the car?'

'I want to piss.' The girl got up, dropping the paper.

'Who's being common now?' Her father tipped the waiter and roared with laughter, his stomach joggling as though it had a life apart. Matilda let out a sigh as the party left. Hugh was choking with laughter.

'How can you laugh?' Then she joined him, enjoying the food and the wine, the pleasure of being taken out to lunch, sitting in the sun.

'I'd never thought of you as attractive to stout matrons.' Matilda looked across at Hugh. The sun had caught his nose, turning it red. 'If you go on sitting in the sun your nose will peel.'

'Mustn't have that. Have you got any sun stuff? I can't afford to draw attention to it.'

Matilda fished in her bag, found a tube of Ambre Solaire. 'Try that.'

'Hugh squeezed a blob onto his finger and applied it to his nose. 'Thanks.' He gestured to the waiter for the bill. 'Let's go and swim. Will you take me to your death beach?'

'It's a long walk.'

'Our lunches can settle before we swim, then we won't get cramp.'

Driving to the cliff, walking down the steep path to the beach, Matilda felt a surge of happiness. She called cheerfully to Folly who raced up and down the path, passing so close to their feet that she nearly tripped them.

'It's a golden afternoon.'

Hugh nodded, enjoying the moment, the pretty dog, the sun, the sea. Matilda ran barefoot on the sand at the cliff bottom, racing along to the flat rock she considered hers. They sat in the sun before undressing and Matilda, remembering the young people's barbecue, told Hugh about it.

'There was a girl who kept saying "super", everything was "super". They wanted me to go away so that they could use this rock. If it hadn't been for them I shouldn't have met you. I had my picnic with me, I was going to swim out.'

'From here?'

'Yes. See that smooth bit of water? That's the current. It carries you out past the lighthouse. Tom was caught in it once. He was lucky, he was picked up by a boat.'

'What was the plan? You've never told me.'

'To eat my Brie and rolls, swallow my pills, wash them down with Beaujolais, then I reckon I could just make the water. The current would have done the rest. The tide has to be exactly right.'

'Drowned people look disgusting.'

'Not like Ophelia?'

'Not one bit. The body bloats.'

'I shall be picked up long before I swell up. One of the fishing boats will find me.'

'Horrible for them.'

'Oh rubbish,' said Matilda. 'They'll enjoy it, tell their friends about it in the pub. I reckon my carcass is worth lots of rounds of drinks.'

'Have you ever seen a dead body?'

'I don't think I have. Let's swim.' Hugh ran down the beach into the water and swam.

'Put my foot in it,' Matilda said to Folly. 'He's seen his mother's. Sit by our clothes, there's a good dog.'

Folly wagged humbly and stayed watching anxiously as Matilda walked down to the water.

Matilda swam, watching Hugh's head moving away from her. 'Dear God,' she said aloud. 'I've put ideas into his head, he won't come back, he's gone.' She called loudly and waved her arm. 'Hugh, come back!' He swam on, his head growing smaller on her horizon. A small wind sprang up, flipping the sea into waves. 'Hugh!' Matilda called. 'Hugh!' A wave filled her mouth, making her gag.

Matilda was further from the beach than she thought. She swam back, her arms and legs tiring. She could see Folly down by the water's edge, advancing, then retreating from the waves, giving small anxious barks.

'Damn him, damn him, damn him!' Matilda cursed Hugh as she pushed her arms through the water. 'Damn him, oh damn him!'

'The wind's getting up.' Hugh swam alongside. 'Sea's getting quite choppy.'

Matilda did not answer. When her feet touched bottom she waded ashore, spitting out the taste of salt, pushing her hair away from her face with wet hands.

'Now what's she on about?' Hugh greeted Folly who jumped and cavorted in the shallows. 'Think we'd get drowned, did you, you foolish little creature.' He watched Matilda walking up to the rock, reach for her towel, rub her face with it, pressing it against her eyes.

'Lovely that was.' He joined her. 'This rock's quite hot.' He sat down and let the water run down him. Matilda, angry with herself, did not speak rubbing herself dry. 'Look the other way. I want to strip,' she said tersely.

Hugh, leaning back on his arms, looked out to sea. He could hear her pulling down the bathing dress and the rubbing of the towel. He glanced along the beach.

'Here come our lunchtime neighbours.' He looked round at Matilda standing naked beside him, rubbing her hair with the towel. With her arms raised her breasts looked quite girlish. She had a flat stomach.

'Oh Christ! Not them again!' Matilda grabbed her knickers. 'I'm used to having this beach to myself. Nobody ever used to come here.'

'I bet fat Dad saw your bush, it's very pretty.'

'Don't be common.' Matilda imitated the girl's voice. 'It's common to talk about bushes. I have grey hairs in it.'

'Distinguished. I didn't note your wrinkled bottom.'

'I'm wrinkled all over. Neck, face, hands, bottom, all wrinkled through to my soul.'

'I must be short-sighted.'

Matilda struggled into her shirt and jeans. 'Put your glasses on, for God's sake. That woman thinks you're attractive in your photographs, she'll recognize you.'

'Does it matter?'

'Don't let's give her the pleasure.'

'The father and mother are sitting down. The girl's going to swim.'

'Let's go. Do get dressed.'

'All right.' He stood up.

'D'you think they heard me calling?' Matilda was suddenly anxious.

'Did you call?'

'Yes. Didn't you hear? I thought you were going out too far.'

'I didn't hear. What did you say?'

'I shouted, "Hugh, Hugh, come back." They could have heard.'

'Suppose they did?'

'That woman knows you are called Hugh. Do hurry.'

'Hurrying would be the stupidest thing. You go ahead if you're nervous.'

'All right.' Carrying her towel and bathing dress in one hand, her shoes in the other, she started along the beach, taking a line which would bring her close to the family party.

The father lay back, his head on his arms, eyes closed, his stomach a mound above skinny legs. The mother sat upright, glancing about her. The girl carefully oiled her arms and legs. She had rather bony knees.

Matilda, walking silently, strained her ears.

'No, dear, I don't suppose so. I only said it's funny he should be called Hugh, that's what she was calling, dear, she was calling "Hugh". I told you. Hush, here she comes.'

'Oh Mummy, don't keep saying "dear", can't you say "darling" or Inez?'

'That Dereck you are going to marry is supposed to be so democratic. Why should he mind if I talk common? If I want to call you "dear" I shall. "Darling" doesn't come naturally to me, you know that. You used to say it was the thing to be common.'

'Oh Mummy, that was in Nigel's day.'

'I only said it was a funny thing that that man over there who looks like the Matricide should be called Hugh, dear. That's all. It's his name, Hugh Warner, it's been in all the papers.'

'Hardly likely he'd be using his own name, is it?' Dad looked up at the sky.

'The *Express* says he's in Paris and has grown a beard.' The girl had turned sulky.

'You can't believe all you read in the papers, dear.'

'Oh Mummy,' the girl almost screamed in desperation. 'Must you say "dear" all the time?'

'Now then, Inez, don't you be rude to your Ma.' Dad sat up and glared at his daughter. 'We've been "dear" to each other all our lives and "dear" we shall stay. We may be common but we are dear to one another and you are dear to us. Eh, Ma, how's that?'

As she pulled on her espadrilles, Matilda listened anxiously.

'It's a very common name.' The girl poured oil into her palm and massaged her throat upwards. 'Think of all the radio and TV Hughs, Hugh and Huw.'

'You contradict everything I say, dear. It's becoming a habit.'

'I wasn't contradicting, I just said –'

'Did your paper say what the chap who ate his wife's doggy-woggy is being charged with?' Dad spoke with his eyes shut. Matilda blessed him.

'Eating dogs isn't a chargeable offence. I asked Dereck.'

'Your Dereck knows it all.'

'Dereck says that bride who vanished from the beach

183

had probably been murdered. That's what Dereck says.'

'Beaches aren't all that safe then. Better be careful when you honeymoon on the Costa what's it, Inez girl.'

'Oh, Daddy.'

'Call me "Dad" like you always have. I don't like this "Daddy" bit, it stinks.'

'Yes, dear, call your Dad "Dad". No need to change all of a sudden now you are engaged to Dereck. Call him "Dad" like always, dear.'

'Oh, Mummy,' the girl whined in exasperation.

'Just because he works in a solicitor's office and talks posh doesn't mean he knows it all. Call your Dad "Dad", dear.'

Matilda, moving away, detected hurt in the mother's voice, then suddenly aggression. 'I'm not saying anything against your Dereck, but we all know people can take elocution lessons.' Matilda risked a backward glance at Inez's angry mother. 'You call us Mum and Dad like you always have. Dear.'

Matilda moved on, her heart thumping. She started up the cliff, daring to look back. She was appalled to see Hugh talking to the family party.

'Is he quite crazy?'

Presently they all laughed and Hugh walked on towards her, followed by Folly.

'Are you quite mad?'

'No. The mother accosted me, said I looked like the Matricide, was I often mistaken for him.'

'Christ! What did you say?'

'I asked, in my best German accent, who was the Matricide? They told me. I made a joke and we all laughed. That's all.'

'They must have heard you talking English at lunch.'

'I doubt it. We never raised our voices. I was on the far side of the table. We listened to them, not they to us.'

'I pray you are right.'

'Don't be so panicky and spoil the afternoon.'

'Sorry. It's been lovely.' Hugh stood looking down at the beach.

'My mother would have loved this beach. She adored places like this.'

'Your *mother*?'

'Just because I killed my mother doesn't mean I don't know what she liked,' Hugh said coldly, looking at Matilda with dislike. 'I know very well what gave her pleasure – pain, fear.'

'Let's get back to the car.' Matilda shivered. 'I'm afraid. That woman heard me call "Hugh". I'm afraid.'

'Yes, she mentioned that. I said "Hugo" was my name. Sounds much the same when shouted. My mother used to call "Hugh-o"? A sort of yodel.'

'You loved your mother?'

'Of course I did.'

'I'm afraid.'

'That's life. All your claptrap about death is rubbish.'

'No, no, it isn't, wasn't.'

Hugh walked ahead to the car. His back view expressed annoyance. Matilda cheered up on the way home, and sang as she drove.

> 'I paid a shilling to see
> A tattooed Lady
> Ta ta-ta ta-ta ta

I can't remember the words. D'you know them?'

'No.'

'I remember, it ends like this –

> On her hips were battleships
> Oh my, but they were fine,'

Matilda sang, 'and

> Right down her spine
> Were the King's own guard in line.

Oh, I have it all wrong. I wish I could remember. Joyce Grenfell sang it at a troops' concert in 1939. I don't suppose you were born.'

'Not quite. Go on singing.'

185

'I'll try and remember the words. My Pa was in the Territorials. Ma took me to their concert.'

'It sounds Edwardian. Go on singing. I like it.'

'I forget the words, just as I forget my life, huge chunks of it.'

'It will all flash before your eyes out by the lighthouse.'

'Maybe. That's something I hadn't thought of. Surely I shall think of something more profound than tattooed ladies?'

'You will think of your lovers, perhaps.' Hugh, lolling beside her, thought of her standing naked, arms raised, on the beach. 'You must have had plenty.'

'No, I didn't. Vague experiments, then I married Tom.'

'But surely –'

'I was faithful.'

'Prig.' Hugh teased. Matilda frowned.

'I was, I promise. No chance of anything else. Tom was a jealous man, he chased other men away. We lived like swans. They mate for life,' she said, knowing she lied.

'Swans,' Hugh jeered.

'I know, I've found out haven't I? But I don't suppose I would have been any different if I had known it all.'

'But since his death?'

'I'm too old. No one. Well, a glint in Mr Jones's eyes soon doused.'

'Well I never.' Hugh thought of the tussling Mr Jones in bed. 'I daresay he'd put up a creditable performance. Maybe you're not keen though.'

'Keen on what?'

'Bed.'

'I adore fucking,' Matilda said intensely. Hugh raised his eyebrows, looking at her sidelong, full mouth, small chin. She opened the mouth and sang, repeating the words she could remember.

'I paid a shilling to see
A tattooed lady,'

then, breaking into a piercing whistle she turned the car off the main road and drove through the lanes to the cottage.

186

'It's been a lovely day. Thanks.'

'I enjoyed it.'

'Here we are. Where's Gus?'

'Can't see him.' Hugh gathered up their bathing things. 'I'll hang these up.'

'Okay. Gus, Gus, where are you? Gus? Sometimes he goes down the river. He always comes back.'

'You sure?'

'Yes.'

'I have to see Mr Jones. I won't be long.'

'Don't let anyone see you.'

'Of course not.' Hugh went up to his room, took his money from the dressing-table drawer. He counted a hundred pounds in notes, put them in his wallet, then counted the rest. Matilda was in the garden picking vegetables. From time to time she called, 'Gus, Gus, come on boy,' in a high voice.

'He'll come, he does this sometimes. It's his way of asserting his independence.'

'You sure?'

'Yes, quite. Don't be long. I'm hungry.'

'Not long –' Hugh walked along the stream, through the copse, followed by Folly, to Mr Jones's bungalow. Mr Jones was sitting in his porch smoking.

'I didn't know you smoked.'

'Pot.' Mr Jones offered the cigarette to Hugh who drew on it deeply. 'Improves the view,' Mr Jones said, 'makes things twice as clear, if you want clarification.'

'I've brought the money.' Hugh gave back the cigarette, handed over the envelopes. Mr Jones counted, then said,

'Okay, fine. I have francs, dollars, deutschmarks, that do you?'

'Yes, thank you.'

'Hold this.' He gave Hugh the joint. 'Won't be long.' He went into the bungalow. Hugh smoked quietly until Mr Jones came back.

'Here you are.' He handed Hugh an envelope. 'That should keep you going for a while. When are you off?'

'Soon.'

'Right. No need to tell me. Does she know?'

'Matilda?'

'Yes.'

'I haven't told her. I'm just going to be there one minute, gone the next.'

'That's the best way.' Mr Jones nodded. 'The *Express* says you've been seen in Paris, the *Mirror* says East Berlin, they're always keen on East Berlin, it's not easy to check.'

'I shall leave the dog.'

'Sure. Something to remember you by.'

'She won't want to remember me. It's her husband she remembers.'

'That's an illusion.' Mr Jones spat, drew on the last dregs of pot. 'She's conned herself all her life, that woman.'

'She doesn't seem to have had much life. I must go.' Hugh stood up quickly. 'She's cooking supper. It's getting dark.'

'Autumn's here –'

'Yes, nearly.'

'Where shall you go?'

'East Berlin.'

Mr Jones waved as Hugh left. As he walked away he could hear him chuckling.

The cottage was strangely still. Hugh paused, smelling danger. Matilda was silent. There was no car by the gate but something had gone wrong. Hugh gestured to Folly to run ahead. The dog trotted along the brick path and in at the kitchen door.

Inside the house Matilda made a noise, just a noise barely human. He ran into the house. Matilda looked up at him. 'The police –'

Hugh felt his heart constrict, sweat break out, pins and needles in his fingers. 'Where? When?'

'They saw him from their car, they tried, one of them went into the water and got wet. There was nothing they could do. His head was bitten off.'

'What are you talking about?'

'Gus. He's dead. A fox, they said. A struggle by the river. His body was in the water. Feathers on the bank, they said. He must have put up a fight.'

Hugh let out his breath. 'Where is he?'

'They took him away. I wouldn't want to see him like that, they said. He pecked one of them once. I thought they were coming for you, but it was Gus. What shall I do?'

Hugh moved, picked up Matilda in his arms and held her close.

'Shut up. Don't speak.' He carried her upstairs. She was lighter than she looked. He pulled off her clothes, snapping buttons, yanking her arms out, unzipped her jeans, pulled them off.

'What are you doing?'

'Undressing you.'

'Why?'

'Shut up.' He kicked off his shoes, tore off his trousers, 'Come here, hold on, open your legs –'

'I –'

'You like fucking, you said so, shut up.' He put his hand over her mouth. 'There, be quiet, just move a bit – there.'

Matilda came alive, gasping, struggling, fighting, joining in, holding him, her response sudden, silent. Then she sighed.

'It hurt, it hurt, you raped me.'

'I didn't mean to rape you. I meant to console.'

'Like your mother,' Matilda murmured.

'What?'

'Nothing. It hurt nicely.'

'You haven't for so long. It will be better next time.' He held her, stroking her back. Outside the room Folly yawned and stretched then, with a sigh, fell asleep. They would remember her dinner in time. She wasn't all that hungry though it was late.

Owls on their silent hunting zoomed over the fields. Holiday makers drove along the main road, making for the motorway and urban life.

Matilda lay in Hugh's arms. 'You will flash before my eyes,' she murmured.

189

'Hush.' He kissed her mouth gently.

'I am old enough to be your mother.' He kissed her, running his tongue along her teeth as a child rattles railings with a stick. 'A good joke. Sleep now, it's not the moment to say so.'

'Would I have liked your mother?'

'I think so. Sleep.' He kissed her.

He slid out of bed, dressed, crept downstairs. His wallet was on the kitchen table. He crept up again for his passport and small bag of clothes, stood by Matilda's door listening.

Matilda snored.

Downstairs Hugh fed Folly, scooping dog meat from a tin, watching her wolf it.

'Quick now, have a run.' He let her into the garden to pee. 'Hurry up.' She came in. 'Stay now. Take good care of her. Be a good dog. Go to your basket.' He pointed to the basket. The dog went to it, sat uneasily, watching as he swallowed a quick sandwich and drank milk. He patted her once. 'Lie down, be good. Take care of her.'

He let himself out by the kitchen door, closing it gently. If he walked fast he could catch the 11.30 to London. Then who knows, he thought. Who knows where my dollars, deutschmarks and francs will take me. From London I can take the tube to Heathrow, into the world, back to life. Walking fast across country, Hugh thought bitterly of his mother and of Matilda. She always hoped I'd find a woman I could love. Now, he thought, pausing by a gate, leaning his head in his arms, thinking of Matilda, now I can't have her. They shan't find me, not now, not ever, for her sake they must not. He hurried on, across the main road, down a side road to the town, to the station. He was engrossed by Matilda, her body and his joined, smelling her, hearing her, feeling her. He did not hear the squeak of brakes or the yelp as a car driving fast clipped Folly on the head and killed her, tossing her body to the curb. He was so absorbed by Matilda that it had not occurred to him that Folly would leap out of the kitchen window and follow.

I will write from wherever I may be, he thought, thinking aloud as people do under stress. I will tell her everything and she will laugh. It will be good for her to remember me with laughter. She needs laughter.

At the station he bought a ticket to Paddington and fell asleep as the train drew out of the station.

Folly's body was hit by two more cars before she was found by the police, squashed flat. 'Poor Mrs Pollyput,' said the constable. 'First that gander, now this. She isn't in luck exactly.'

26

Waking, hearing the birds, Matilda stretched, then curled up again. She wanted to prolong her sense of ease. She felt as though each bit of her body was free from the tension which had been there so long. She felt the bed beside her. Hugh had gone. It didn't matter. A wren sang loudly in the garden. He would come back. There would be more. She tried to remember whether it had ever been like that with Tom. It hadn't. Good but not perfect. Hugh was so much younger than she, it couldn't last. He would go away, indeed he must go away otherwise sooner rather than later he would be in prison. She slept a little then woke, thinking of Gus.

No more honking, no more slap of feet, no more throttling noises, no more messes. She felt calm now, her horror and grief over his death had raised her emotions to the pitch which had allowed love. By Gus's death I am complete, she thought. It was pleasant to stretch her legs without disturbing a dog. Since Stub's death she had slept alone. Folly had slept lately with Hugh, she was his dog. Matilda hoped Hugh had fed her during the night. She remembered him leaving. He would have fed her surely. The police had been kind about Gus, nice of them to come and tell her, they might easily have telephoned or done nothing. It was lucky they had not run into Hugh, that he was out when they came.

Matilda remembered the two policemen. She had guessed that Gus lay headless in their Panda car. She had guessed too that one of the policemen would give the body to his wife and that Gus would be roasted and

192

eaten. She was not shocked or angry about this, it seemed natural. She thought again of Hugh and, turning away from the light, thought he must be sleeping deeply after so much – she searched for the right word – expenditure. Yes, a great night of spending. She smiled, pulling the sheet up over her eyes, dozing, conscious of happiness. She must guard it.

At the police station the two constables from the Panda car made their report. The sergeant made notes.

'Okay, just an ordinary night.'

'Do we still keep an eye open for the fellow who killed his old mother?'

'Nothing come through to the contrary. That missing bride is more urgent.'

'Seems a waste of time.'

'Putting the public's back up. Every man with a large nose is feeling awkward,' said the younger constable.

'You've got a large nose, Sergeant,' ventured his mate.

'I know that. That's why the public has my sympathy for once. The moment I'm in civvies I feel awkward. My wife says people stare.'

'They stare because you're such a fine upstanding man, Sergeant, not because of your hooter.'

'Enough of that.'

'Okay, Sarge, what about the dog, then? What do we do?'

'The goose was last night, wasn't it?'

'Yes.'

'You passing her way as you go off duty?'

'No, we aren't.'

'Well pass her way, take her the dog, tell her before you go off duty.'

'That's overtime.'

'No it isn't.' The sergeant wrote up a note. 'That's paying for the goose. It's my guess one of you is going to eat it.'

'Very well, Sergeant.' The two policemen went out.

'Crafty bastard. My Annie says with an old bird, boil it first, then roast it slow and it will taste like a young one.

She knows a thing or two. She was brought up on a farm.'

'Lot to be said for country lore.' The second policeman, who was courting a secretary in the Council Offices, slipped the car into gear. 'Seems stupid though to me.'

'What does?'

'We keep the bird and you eat it but the dog, which is much more of a mess, we return.'

'You don't licence a goose and you can't eat dog.'

'They do in China.'

'I know that. Let's get it over with. I hate this kind of job. Who is this Mrs Pollyput anyway?'

'They've lived here a long time. He died a few years back. She doesn't mix much. Got grown children. They never come to see her. He ran some sort of travel business from home. Never been any trouble there apart from the odd motoring offence. She doesn't belong to the W.I. or go to church. She's not above the occasional coarse expression. Talks to herself and sings too. It's her time of life, I suppose.'

'My Mum's having hot flushes.'

'There you are then.'

'And here we are. You carry the dog and I'll do the talking.'

'That isn't fair.'

'Isn't it? Afraid of messing your uniform? It's in a sack isn't it? Hold it well away from you so it won't drip. You carry the dog, you're eating the goose.'

'We could share it.'

'Oh belt up. I don't fancy it.'

Matilda heard a car door slam and, shortly after, a knock on the door. She got out of bed and looked from her window.

'You again? I'm asleep, can't you bugger off?' Her voice rose high.

'Sorry, Mrs Pollyput, but –'

'Wait a minute, I'll come down.' She withdrew her head.

'You're right, she is coarse.'

'Told you so.' They stood patiently.

Matilda's knees trembled as she pulled on Anabel's dressing-gown, ran a comb through her hair. She looked at the clock.

'Christ, it's late. What an oversleeping.'

She took a deep breath, put the comb down, pulled the sash of the dessing-gown tight and left the room. Before coming down she looked into Hugh's room, her finger on her lips. It was empty, the bed made.

'Taken Folly out. Please God keep him away while they are here.' She ran downstairs and opened the door.

'What is it?'

'Mrs Pollyput, it's –'

'What is it?'

'Is this your dog, Mrs Pollyput? Found her on the main road. Can't have known what hit her.'

Matilda said nothing.

'Must have been following somebody, she was nearly in the town.'

'Following somebody?'

'That's what the sergeant thinks.'

'Who?'

'Who what, Mrs Pollyput?'

'My name is Mrs Poliport.'

'Yes, Mrs Poliport.'

'Was she seen following somebody? Who would she follow?'

'It was just his idea. We only found her.'

'When?'

'Coming off duty we –'

'You were coming on duty when you found my gander.'

'Yes Mrs Pollyput, Poliport.'

'Yes, she's my dog.' Matilda put out a hand to touch the mangled body. 'She's cold.'

'Er, yes.'

'This is an idiot conversation. Where did you say you found her?'

'On the main road by the turning to the station.'

'The turning to the station. I see.' Matilda was quite

195

still. The policemen stood embarrassed.

'You all right, Mrs Poliport?'

'Would you be?' Matilda stared at him. 'Give her to me.' The younger policeman made a protesting noise.

'Give her to me.' Matilda took hold of the body in the sack, holding it close.

'Following somebody.'

'Or running away. She may have been frightened. Dogs get scared on roads, Mrs Poliport.'

'Yes.'

'You all right, Mrs Poliport? Would you like us to make you some tea?'

'No thank you. I must buy some Brie and a bottle of Beaujolais.'

'What, Mrs Poliport?'

'Cheese and wine –' Matilda stood staring at them, her face white, 'not tea.'

'Oh. You sure you're all right? We could –'

'You couldn't do anything. Just bugger off.' She turned into the house, shutting the door in their faces. The two men exchanged glances, one of them took off his hat, resettled it on his head. The other straightened his tunic. They turned to go. Matilda opened the door and shouted, 'He'll make very tough eating,' and slammed it again. They heard her scream 'Cannibals!'

'Phew!'

'Holy Cow!' They drove off.

'Hot flush or no hot flush, she's put me off my dinner. Bugger off, is it? The sergeant can go himself another time.'

'Funny her being in bed this time of the morning. She's usually up at dawn, everybody knows that.'

'Perhaps she had some fella for the night.'

'Don't be daft – at her age?'

'Daresay it was just shock. She hasn't had that dog long, only bought it a licence the other day, she told me. I told her it wasn't yet six months and not to worry.'

'Wasted her lolly then.'

27

When her arms began to ache, Matilda put the sack down on the kitchen table. The clock said midday. She went across the room and wound it. She felt dizzy and put out her hand to steady herself against the Rayburn. It was cold. She looked in the firebox. The draught she made opening the stove stirred the embers. As she straightened up she saw the mess on her dressing-gown. She took it off and wrapped it round Folly's body. The rather tarty chiffon and lace garment which had once belonged to Anabel made a neat wrapping. Realizing she was naked she went upstairs and ran the bath very deep and hot. She washed thoroughly and shampooed her hair, ducking under the water to rinse it.

She dressed in the jeans and shirt she found on her bedroom floor. There was only the top button left, the others twinkled up from the carpet. She pulled on a sweater, combed her wet hair, put on espadrilles, went back to the bathroom to clean her teeth. As she brushed them she noticed that Hugh's shaving things were gone from the shelf, that his sponge was gone and his tooth-brush.

She looked at her reflection in the mirror without recognition.

From the garden shed she fetched fork and spade and dug a deep hole by the rhubarb bed where the ground was soft and free of stones. When it was deep enough she fetched Folly and laid her in the hole, covered it with earth and trod it flat. Her espadrilles were full of grit and she had hurt the sole of her foot, digging. She took

off the espadrilles, shook out the grit, then walked awkwardly to the tool shed, carrying the shoes in one hand,
the fork and spade in the other. Her hand was not large
enough to hold the tools; she dropped the spade with a
clatter, bruising her foot. She hung the tools on their
hooks and closed the shed door.

'Matilda. I heard. I came to see whether I could help.'
Mr Jones stood a few yards off.

'Excuse me, I've just had a bath. My hair is wet.'

'I heard about Gus and Folly. I wondered –'

'Yes?'

'Is there anything I can do?'

'Do you have a large flat stone?'

'I can bring you a slab from my path, one of the paving
stones.'

'Could you bring it at once?'

'Yes, of course. You look strange. Shall I make you
some tea?'

'Not tea!' Matilda exclaimed harshly.

'I'll get the stone at once.'

'Please do.'

'I'm sorry.'

'Sorry to be rude. It's just –'

'I know. I'll go and get it.'

Mr Jones broke into a trot, running towards his bungalow. Matilda thought he looked ridiculous from behind.
Short, fat, middle-aged men should not run.

She went back to the house to wash her hands at the
sink, cleaning the earth from under her nails with an
orange stick. There was a stain on the kitchen table. She
wiped it with a wet cloth.

Waiting for Mr Jones, Matilda wandered round the
house. Everything was in its place. The spiders were
back slung across ceiling corners. She left them alone.

In her room she made the bed, smoothing the stained
sheets, pulling up the blankets, puffing up the pillows.
She held her breath so that she would not smell what
was there, covered the whole with the patchwork
bed spread Claud had sent from America. 'Pretty.'

198

She stroked it. 'Sweet Claud.'

Hugh's room was empty. She inspected for traces of his occupancy. There were none.

Mr Jones came with a stone slab in his arms.

'Will this do? It's Delabole slate.'

'Yes, it will. Thank you.'

Together they went to the dog's grave.

'Where shall I put it?'

'Here, across here.' Matilda pointed.

Mr Jones laid the stone, rocking it to level the earth.

'Thank you,' she said again.

'It's nothing. Can I do anything else?'

'No thank you. I have to go out and shop.'

'Could I not do it for you? You should rest.'

'No thank you. I'm going for a swim.'

Mr Jones stood looking miserably at Matilda.

'I know Hugh has gone.'

'Yes.'

'He meant you to keep Folly.'

'She was his dog. She followed him – naturally.'

'He wouldn't have wanted her to.'

'I daresay not. I don't think it matters now what he wanted, not any more, not now.'

'He would have wanted to leave you happy.'

'Don't talk drivel.'

'I'm sorry. I – I wanted.'

'You *what?*'

'I wanted to tell you I love you, Matilda. I always have. I want to comfort you. I'd like to begin by making you some tea.'

'I don't want tea, Mr Jones. It's very kind of you but I don't need comforting. I don't think you do love me, it's just an idea, all in the mind.'

'It's not only in my mind, it's in my balls.' Mr Jones found himself shouting at Matilda, longing to hit her.

'It makes no odds to me whether your love is up or down, Mr Jones. I'm sorry, I have to go out.' Matilda moved towards the house.

'I chose the wrong moment. I thought we could live

199

here in your house or in my bungalow –'

'Oh, fuck your bungalow!'

'All right. I'm sorry. I'll go.'

Mr Jones turned and went. Matilda watched him go out of sight, fetched her towel and bathing dress from the line, noting that Hugh had even remembered to take his swimming trunks, which had belonged, she thought resentfully, to Tom.

She looked in her bag to see if she had any money. Hugh might have taken that too, but her purse was full. She put it in the beach bag with the towel and the bathing dress, went out, locked the door, put the key under the doorstep, got into the car and drove off to the town.

It was market day so she had trouble finding a place to park the car, finally leaving it on a double yellow line.

She made for the wine shop where she bought a bottle of Beaujolais, then to the baker where she bought rolls. At the delicatessen she persuaded the girl behind the counter who was more than usually busy to butter the rolls while she chose some Brie.

'What d'you want to do that for? A whole crowd of people are waiting,' the man who owned the shop hissed at his assistant as she buttered the rolls.

'She had a funny look in her eye. I didn't like to say no.'

'Don't let me catch you at it again. Here you are, Madam.' He handed the Brie in its paper bag to Matilda. 'Glad to be of assistance.'

'I don't suppose she'll ask me again, she never has before.' The girl watched Matilda leave the shop.

'Did she pay for the butter?'

'Paid for half a pound and only wanted what I used on the rolls. I think she's a nutter.'

There was a ticket under the windscreen wiper of the car. Matilda handed it to a passer-by, who examined it, puzzled, then shouted, 'Hey!' as she drove away without looking back.

Parking the car at the usual place, she sauntered along the cliff path, looking down at the sea, which was calm but grey. The beach was empty, the season over.

She was glad she had her sweater, wished she was wearing socks. It was chilly and her foot bruised where she had dropped the spade. She sang softly going down the cliff path:

'I paid a shilling to see
A tattooed La-a-dy.'

Reaching the sand, she kicked off her espadrilles, leaving them to lie, hurrying barefoot to the far end of the beach to the flat rock.

'And right down her spine
Were the King's Own Guard in line.'

The rock was cold when she sat on it. She shivered, unpacking the rolls and Brie, standing the Beaujolais carefully so that it would not topple over. She felt in the bag for the corkscrew.

'Oh God! I've left it behind.' She began to weep. 'It's got to be there –' She tipped the bag over, shaking it. No corkscrew. A sheet of paper slid to her feet.

Darling Matilda. Hugh's writing, a little blurred by the damp towel. *I love you. I can't impose my life on yours. I must go away. I love you. You are the kind of woman my mother would have loved. You are what I have wanted, what she wanted for me. I thought she knew nothing of love, was old, naïve. Christ, this is an impossible letter to write. Forgive me. Folly will look after you, hook on to her. She belongs to us both, just hook on. Killing my mother was an accident. She was terrified of mice. Don't laugh. There was a mouse on the sofa. She cried to me for help. I smashed at it with the tray as she moved. I've been too embarrassed to tell anyone. Please don't laugh, though I love your laughter. Hugh.*

Matilda tore the letter, letting the breeze scatter the pieces. She undressed, pulling on her swimsuit, goose pimples on her legs. Sitting on the rock she reached in her bag for the pills, spilled them into her hand. She knocked the neck of the bottle against the rock, crammed her mouth full of pills, choking them down with the wine. The jagged glass cut her mouth. She poured in more pills, more wine.

The tide was just right, on the turn, the sea waiting. Matilda stood up.

'Folly?' she called, feeling dizzy, 'belongs to us both?' She fell on her knees, crawling down the beach on all fours. 'Gus?' She retched, keeping the pills down with an effort. 'We all belong to you,' she whispered, reaching the water. 'I'm coming.'

A gull swooped down to snatch a roll from the rock, followed by others, screaming, fighting, white wings beating, yellow eyes glinting, beaks snatching.

The sea caught Matilda as she began to swim out. She did not wish to get her hair wet.

It's late in the year for swimming. She pushed her arms out mechanically, turning the grey water pink with the blood from her mouth. A memory came tentatively. She had read or heard that people shit as they die. In distress she pulled off her swimsuit, getting her hair wet as she did so. She let the thing drift away.

At least I shall die with my body clean. She swam more slowly now. I should see my past life flash before my eyes. Her wounded mouth smiled. A memory which had so long eluded her came uselessly back. John/Piers in Trafalgar Square, his bowler, his umbrella. Whose party had he taken her to? Some place in Bloomsbury. I got drunk, she remembered, swimming very slowly now, never been drunk before. He had taken her into a bedroom. She had smelled his hair oil from Trumpers.

She had pushed it out of her mind. 'Hugh,' she called in the cold tide, 'Hugh, I want to tell you –' John/Piers next honours list had pushed her onto a bed, pulled up her skirt, hadn't even pulled off her knickers.

'This will be a new sensation.' That voice of his.

'Death you are new too,' she said to the tide.

The fishing boat found the body floating by the light-house.

202

'Looks as though she's laughing,' the younger man said.

'Cut her mouth on the rocks,' said his father. 'Haul it in. Cover it with a bit of tarpaulin, 'tisn't decent, not as though she were young.'

'Buggered up a day's fishing, this.'

THE END

MARY WESLEY

A Sensible Life

'A splendid novel'
Evening Standard

Flora Trevelyan is a ten-year-old misfit, despised by her selfish and indolent parents, and left to wander the streets of a small French town whilst her parents prepare to depart for life in colonial India. There she befriends the locals, acquires an extensive vocabulary of French foul language and encounters the privileged lifestyle of the elegant middle-class British families holidaying in 1920s France. Introduced for the first time to kindly, civilised and, above all, caring people Flora falls helplessly and hopelessly in love with not one but three young men.

Over the next forty years Flora will grow from an awkward schoolgirl into a stunning beauty and explore, consummate and finally resolve each of these affairs.

'She writes with the knowledge and wisdom of serene old age and the emotional exuberance of glowing young womanhood'
Daily Telegraph

'Made me both laugh out loud and cry'
Philip Howard, *The Times*

VINTAGE BOOKS
London

MARY WESLEY

The Camomile Lawn

'The Camomile Lawn provides equal doses of sex and repression in war-torn Britain with panache and pace'

The Times

It is August, 1939 and five cousins have gathered at their aunt's house in Cornwall for their annual summer holiday and ritual 'Terror Run'. There is nineteen-year-old Oliver, back from fighting in the Spanish Civil War and desperately in love with the beautiful but grasping Calypso; brother and sister Polly and Walter; and ten-year-old Sophie, orphaned at birth and unloved by her aunt and uncle. By the end of the evening war will have been declared and the lives of all five cousins will have been altered irrevocably.

The Camomile Lawn follows the cousins through the war and beyond, into adulthood and old age, united by shared losses and lovers, by family ties and friends. As each of them grows up they fight not just to survive but to remain true to themselves and to those they love.

'A very good book indeed...Rich in detail, careful and subtle in observation, mature in judgement'

Susan Hill

VINTAGE BOOKS

London

BY MARY WESLEY
ALSO AVAILABLE FROM VINTAGE

☐ The Camomile Lawn	0099499142	£7.50
☐ Not That Sort of Girl	0099499126	£7.50
☐ A Sensible Life	0099499134	£7.50

FREE POST AND PACKING
Overseas customers allow £2.00 per paperback

BY PHONE: 01624 677237

BY POST: Random House Books
C/o Bookpost, PO Box 29, Douglas
Isle of Man, IM99 1BQ

BY FAX: 01624 670923

BY EMAIL: bookshop@enterprise.net

Cheques (payable to Bookpost) and credit cards accepted

Prices and availability subject to change without notice.
Allow 28 days for delivery.
When placing your order, please mention if you do not wish to receive
any additional information.

www.randomhouse.co.uk/vintage